My deepest gratitude to David Sunderland for proofreading this book, to Andrea Luz Sanchez for making its beautiful cover and to Paula Matczyńska for her inspiration.

Juan Martin Sánchez is an Argentinean writer whose books touch upon love, society and the meaning of life in a romantic realist style similar to Dostoevsky's and Tagore's. His novels are set either in Argentina or Poland, where he has lived, and they are full of personal experiences and insights about life disguised in literary form. He's also written *Love in the Time of the Internet* and *Tribulations of People in the World,* as well as some short stories and miscellaneous articles which are available on the blog: Random Reflections on the World.

# Second Chances

by Juan Martin Sanchez

Printed in Poznan, Poland, 2016.

To order additional copies, contact:
soy_juanma86@yahoo.com

# Chapter 1

It was February second in Poznan. The momentary snow had melted away and the winter seemed to be set on being mild that year. Miguel was having a second breakfast: pancake. His pancake was different, though; not the normal thin spongy one, but a rather thick crusty one. This was attained by simply pouring more paste and letting it cook for longer. That's why he called it pancake, in the singular form, because it was just one big and filling pancake, which he'd spread with butter and marmalade to eat with his hands.

On the kitchen table there was an old radio mended with masking tape. The radio had been there for days, but it was the first time Miguel had paid attention to it. "What is so special about it?" he thought, "Just a trademark of third world countries. But is Poland a third world country?" he wondered. "It must be if an obsolete artifact that's meant to be thrown away is allowed to lie in an unsuitable place in inadequate repair. If not a symbol of poverty, it's at least a sign of decadency." That may have been the reason why he was in that country; it made him feel at home.

The pancake was ready; it may have been a little overdone too; its hardness gave away this fact. He'd been watching some reviews of Argentinean films during the morning; he surely was a little nostalgic. Crunching his pancake with butter, he couldn't help recalling the crackers he used to have for breakfast back there. He hadn't seen those in Poland. Was he going to start the melancholic path that would lead him to miss his own country so much that he'd be forced to go back? He hoped not, but he actually had solid reasons not to miss his country.

The following day dawned radiantly. His window faced the east, so he could enjoy the full glow of the rising sun. He had an exam he hadn't studied for; as usual in his life, nothing was studied and nothing had too much effort put into it except literature. Exams could be ignored; work wasn't an immediate need; the only emergency was always loneliness. A lonely soul is capable of dire extremes, especially when it's accompanied by intellectual aloofness and moral detachment. Nothing tied him to this world and he was in constant search of an excuse for living.

Miguel liked starting his days early and with a fast. He was a sleepyhead and he wasn't moderate in eating habits either, so he tried to combat his weaknesses by getting up early. The fasting part was easy; he was never hungry in the morning, since he generally ate late at night. Thus a solemn feeling reigned in his room on his days off, when he sat in front of the computer and ingested some literature accompanied by a cup of tea. His stomach would always let him know when it was time for a bowl of delicious, milky and honeyed oatmeal or one of his big pancakes with butter.

He'd wasted a whole month of his life pining after a girl. She was a musician and she'd left him to pursue her dreams. She'd meant sweetness to him, but her presence in his life had been like a loan from the bank of happiness, with the interest growing exponentially, until he'd been forced to default. Fortunately for him, everything was over and he wasn't inflating his emotional economy any longer.

Whenever Miguel's morale was a little low, he tended to make new acquaintances and be a little more flexible about his interests and his investment of time. He'd met an American evangelist called Steven; he was nice and Miguel could practice his English with him. Besides, he organized homely meetings where Miguel could spend his free Saturday afternoons. He'd invited him over for Bible reading; Miguel had no intention to go, but he was allured by food and the promise of hanging around after the religious task. Miguel was deliberately late, arriving almost at the end of the reading so he could enjoy the food and good company without the burden of the indoctrination. "Religion is for sheep, not for humans," thought Miguel. "People who can think for themselves don't resort to this moral stratagem." Miguel thought of the thousands of years men had lived on earth and the variety of ways in which they'd lived, most of them without the help of the Christian god. "Ancient Greeks were renowned for their knowledge and wisdom, and they weren't under Jehovah's wing," thought Miguel. For him it seemed preposterous to believe that God is the only way to happiness and to try to convince others of this idea, as if the believers' own happiness didn't suffice them but they wanted to force happiness onto everyone else.

Miguel stayed after the bible reading and, after everyone else left, he engaged Steven in a serious conversation. Steven was inclined to answer to all of Miguel's questions, partly because he was doing missionary work in Poland and partly because he was really interested in getting to know him better. For Steven, Miguel represented those people of goodwill who haven't found the path yet, but who strive and are always crying to the Lord inadvertently. Steven remembered his own path towards God and he saw himself years before in Miguel's acts and words. He honestly wanted to help Miguel find peace of mind and happiness; he wasn't recruiting any sheep to his herd, but he was dedicating his time and effort to a selfless cause.

For Miguel, the case was practically closed because he felt that there was no way to agree with an evangelist or to talk them out of their beliefs. He thought that their faith comes from the need to believe itself, even when they try to argue logically. He was sure that the best argument to give to evangelists for not following their advice was simply that their religion is boring and that joy can simply be found in the contemplation of life's miracle. "A personal religion is more necessary than a church, where a bunch of people think they can feel the same and seek faith in the same way," he said bluntly to Steven. Miguel was lying on a sofa, his feet up, showing his old socks to his friend. Steven didn't flinch; Miguel's words didn't astonish him, although he found Miguel's posture too irreverent for a subject like this one. He was sitting straight in a chair two meters and a half away from Miguel, so he projected his voice across the room as if addressing an imaginary audience.

"The church is people who share your views and ideals. You aren't supposed to agree with them blindly but to choose your church carefully. I've been to many congregations; I've been to what Catholics call a church: a building for religious ceremonies; but my church is God's church and He is the ideal I follow now. Other people who follow the same ideal are welcome to my church." said Steven, self-satisfied with his answer.

"I don't believe in God," uttered Miguel faintly, as if he didn't want to fissure his interlocutor's faith with a more assertive utterance. Steven interpreted this deferential tone as a sign of Miguel's moral submission to his judgment, so he welcomed Miguel's straightforwardness instead of being taken aback by such a robust opinion. "You can't not believe in God," he said. 'He is everywhere and everything proves it. The world we live in exists only in God; outside Him there's nothing. Do you believe in nothingness?" That was quite an abrupt and too deep a philosophical question to be answered without deliberation. However, Miguel didn't want to break the flow of thought and, as in chess, in which we are forced to move our pieces even when it's not to our advantage, Miguel decided to move on and see what was next.

"Yes, I believe in nothingness," he said. "I believe we come from nothing and we'll come to an end and be nothing again." Steven was dismayed by this miscarried spark of intellect. He suddenly saw that Miguel was no simple beggar humbling himself in front of him but a sort of intellectual enemy to be defeated. He took his task matter-of-factly, though, because he knew he wasn't fighting the sinner but the sin. He wanted to talk Miguel out of his misconception.

"Nihilism is an impossible stance in life because it leads to death and destruction and not to real creation. Even nihilists like Nietzsche and Sartre must have believed in something to write such imposing works," said Steven assuming that Miguel was acquainted with the works of those philosophers. Miguel had read some of their books, but he didn't immediately see the connection between what he'd said and the nihilistic movement. Besides, from what he knew, Sartre wasn't a nihilist but an

9

existentialist. But he thought that that was the most popular evangelizing method: rough categorization.

"I don't know; I'm not a nihilist," he simply said and the topic was dropped. Steven had realized that he had struck a false note by presenting his conclusions like that. He should have waited until things fell of their own weight. Now that he'd tried to impose a thought on his listener, he knew that he'd only find a defensive attitude. He would have to give up the evangelizing for the time being. They went on talking about lighter topics until they had no more interesting things to say to each other and Miguel took his leave.

Yet Miguel was aware of the fact that this issue had touched him deeply and that he was drawn to these kinds of arguments. The only thing he didn't want was for his interest in these questions to be smothered by blindly following a path marked by someone else. His intelligence didn't allow him to overlook religious people's intellectual loopholes; he couldn't help seeing them as handicapped people that could not stand on their own legs. For sure he didn't find the way sometimes, but he didn't believe that the Christian God was the way either. He believed that only by having faith in himself could he find peace of mind, not by underestimating himself or believing in a godly design for him, but by realizing his talents and limitations and making the best of his life.

*You know as much of feelings*
*and the way they're written*
*as I know of poems*
*and their legitimacy.*
*When you do something*
*you've never dreamed of,*
*and you're just pretending*
*to be yourself for a day,*
*then you'll see how I do*

*to write my verses,*
*from artless honesty,*
*coarse feelings without refinement,*
*drawn from drab reality.*

*Fly, fly butterfly, over the piano,*
*the strings are tense, awaiting your flutter,*
*poise yourself but an instant*
*in every key, and in the wake of your flight*
*notes that wane and are diffused in the air.*
*The strings are ready, the music is waiting*
*for you to stroke it, awake it from slumber,*
*and then again the infinite silence*
*already welcomes your next flight.*

## Chapter 2

Our main enemy is anxiety, Sartre would say. Miguel had the good fortune to meet some beautiful girls who were interested in him, but he gave up easily. He was too forward and he didn't take rejection very well, so he was doomed to bump his head against an ice wall most of the time. Miguel had been infatuated many times and he suddenly recollected the moment in which he met the last girl whom he'd lost his head for, leaving aside the musician. Her name was Hellen. She was dancing freely on the dancefloor, alone, but cheerful. He saw her loneliness in the fact that she overdid her dancing; she was like a baby bursting with merriment at the sight of life's miracle. It was a happy sight except for the fact that it was so out of place, in a nightclub, in a situation where happiness means just the satisfaction you can get from the moment. He saw the cheerfulness in her face, on which a smile spread, when he approached her. She was so natural that his heart melted. Her beauty was roughened by her personality, which was as wild as a bird's. He danced to the rhythm and she freed her body from earthly constraints. He led her and she displayed her charm. Her youth and vigor blossomed for him. He stole kisses from her and she did some dancing tricks for him; both of them made use of their whole weaponry. His world became that girl in that club in a foreign city; his only aim was to take care of her. She was leaving, though, and he had to let her go; he just asked for her phone number and walked along with her till she mingled with the crowd. She was looking for her friend and he started looking for someone else to dance with, or maybe he was just waiting till the adrenaline faded away. But she came back to him; she couldn't find her friend. He helped her look for her and, when he turned his head, she was clung to his lips.

The next time they met it was in a bar downtown. He stood outside waiting for her until he saw her coming. He turned towards her and fixed his eyes on her silhouette emerging from the blend of buildings and people. She greeted him with a smile and they went inside. They were the only ones at the bar; it was too early for regular customers. Miguel was thrown back by Hellen's reserved attitude; she sat minimalistically and didn't look him straight in the eye but rather kept her gaze askew, as if talking to herself rather than to him. The conversation had that tension that's found when two equal spirits meet. She was smart and stubborn; he was arrogant and opinionated. The combination was explosive. However, he could notice that she wasn't the same as she'd been at the club; she was all she'd been before and as sensitive as he'd expected her to be, but she'd put a check on the free flow of her feelings. She was fidgety and he couldn't find a way to make her at ease. He tried putting his hand on her shoulder in a subtle embrace, but she reacted immediately: "I'm not ready for it", she said, and he took his hand away in a gesture full of understanding. However, he didn't understand. What could possibly ail her? The conversation went on, but only about trivial matters, and the ghost that separated them grew larger until he felt alienated from her. Miguel was left with a bitter taste after their meeting, but he wasn't less in

12

love because of that.

"Don't make sirens out of seals," his friend Leo told him. They were sitting at an outdoor bar in the middle of Freedom Square. It was the end of summer and Polish people were profiting from their last sunny days. Leonardo was an Italian engineer living in Poland. He'd met his current girlfriend during one of his trips to the country and he'd settled there in spite of the relatively low income. Leonardo liked coining new sayings and this was his latest one, the exclusive that had been broadcast to his friend: "Don't make sirens out of seals."

"She's a siren; I don't need to make her up," said Miguel, while he distractedly watched the pretty waitress, smiling at a customer from behind the bar.

"What I mean is she's just a girl man, and she kissed you in a club after doing some dirty dance for you; you can't expect chastity from her," said Leo.

Miguel was boiling with wounded pride at hearing the object of his romantic fantasies being desecrated in that way. He coped with it by creating a gap in his mind between him and his friend. The memories he had of the girl weren't consistent with the description of her he was hearing. He knew that everything could be seen from many aspects and, in a different light, something could appear completely different from what it really was, so he let the offense against his girl pass unattended.

"You'll meet many; you know how to dance and girls like that," continued Leonardo patronizingly. "I feel for you, really; I've had my white nights also. But it's not worth talking about it. You must have a winner's mindset or you won't get much out of life, especially out of women. They are a wild bunch, they are, and a pretty cunning one too. However, if you play it cool and strike the right notes they'll come to you like bees to honey; I know what I'm telling you."

Miguel couldn't help noticing the streak of misogyny in his friend's voice and he wondered if real love was possible where contempt was involved.

Miguel didn't mind being rejected by another girl; his problem was that he desired too much and he got excited too easily. His imagination was too powerful and a slight stimulus could unleash it. He was listening attentively to every word, but he was reading too much between the lines, so the conversation was just reinforcing his own ideas.

"Try to ask her out once or twice more and then drop it; she probably isn't interested right now, and if she isn't interested right now she'll never be seriously interested in you. Do you want to be her second choice?" Leo shot this unexpected question at Miguel. Miguel had to make strenuous efforts to gather up his words into a coherent answer which didn't give away the fact that he disregarded completely what his friend was saying. "Well, she's my second, third or I-lost-the-count-which choice too; I've been in love before so I don't expect her..."

"You're just avoiding the point man, so typical of you," interrupted his friend. "Think about it seriously for a moment. You want to have a special girl beside you for the rest of your life, don't you?" The conversation was going in a direction that caught Miguel's interest. He consented with a nod. "Then you want her also to have someone special beside her; it's a principle of reciprocity. If she doesn't feel that you're the best option for her, you just can't think that about her either; otherwise the relationship will be unbalanced and the more you worship her, the more she'll belittle you in her mind." Everything that Miguel was hearing now made sense and he started to be drawn by the magnetic personality and convincing speech of his friend. He felt he had something to lose if he yielded to his friend's ideas, but he had forgotten what it was. The girl he was fighting for seemed to be able to defend herself on her own; she was self-sufficient after all and she'd proven it by not wanting to get involved with him.

"Really man, the girl that's for you will come knocking at your door and shouting at your window; leaving a thousand and one messages on your answer machine," said Leo in a more poetical tone. Miguel couldn't help smiling at the idea of the answer machine; his friend was an engineer and he did not take technological advancements for granted as lay people usually do. His mind and speech were full of old-fashioned machines and short-lived gadgets that had once made life easier for many people. Every time Miguel heard about one of these old artifacts, he couldn't help recalling his old-fashioned country. He felt closer to his friend for having provoked that feeling in him.

"Effortlessness is the rule, remember. No one is going to pay you for your efforts, and one day you'll burst with all the pent-up feelings of unfairness you've accumulated and the girl will just stare at you perplexedly. So the moment to start getting paid for your efforts is the same moment in which you meet a girl. If she doesn't give you any immediate satisfaction, she never will do. Have that always in mind." Leo had started to sound like a scholar to Miguel; he wondered how much effort he had put into developing all these ideas.

"Ok, I understand," reacted Miguel at last. "I'll look for a girl that wants to be with me as much as I want to be with her."

"Right," encouraged Leo. "I'm sure there are plenty of fish you can't see because you're fishing in turbid waters, my friend," he concluded with one of his proverbial phrases. Miguel felt that Leo was bound to be a love guru and that he even had the potential to be a spiritual teacher if he exerted himself.

"Ok, I must leave you; I have to meet my girlfriend at the shoe store. Occupational hazards," said Leo with a half-smile, before he emptied his glass of beer. Miguel empathized with his friend this time; he'd also been to buy shoes and clothing with girls a couple of times and he didn't envy the experience. He walked slowly back home, thinking about Hellen, but more than anything else, thinking about himself.

## Chapter 3

Hellen was dazzling in her black dress and her green stockings. Her shape seemed to be carved in marble, with firm and round contours that were a combination of exercise and good genes. Hellen was a dancer, as evidenced by her sculpted legs. Were it not for her big blue eyes, Miguel wouldn't have found the means to detach his look from her thighs. She had the biggest eyes he'd ever seen, oceanic blue with hues of stormy gray. She was fidgeting with her cellphone while they waited for her order. They'd gone to dance tango at one of those hidden cafes that you discover through a party or event, even though you've passed by them many times. It was a luxurious place, though, and this was probably going to become evident in the bill. Miguel had ordered a glass of wine, to be in tune with the lavish meal and wine ordered by his date. Considering the fact that they'd come to dance, he thought it inconsiderate on her part to have sudden whims for meals and drinks. She'd mentioned she was hungry while they were walking to the place, but when he suggested she should buy a yoghurt or something in a supermarket, she just smiled scornfully. He was obviously in love, for he didn't take notice of that smile just as he wouldn't take notice of having spent fifty zlotys by the end of the night, excluding the tickets for the soiree, which she'd gallantly paid for. Those were trifles when love was at stake, and Miguel didn't have the capacity or the inclination to tar the object of his desire with petty concerns and worldly matters.

It was time to dance and Miguel was anxious to feel her in his arms again. Dancing can be such a trivial thing for most people, but for a sensual spirit like Miguel, there were no limits to the rush of emotion he could feel while holding a beautiful girl in his arms. The usual code system through which people see things was altered in Miguel's brain. Dancing meant no light entertainment or pleasant pastime for him; it was a violent act, a symbol of possession, an atavistic form of social interaction or rather a primeval manifestation of feelings.

That's why Miguel couldn't be bothered with steps or figures; his dance was rhythm, the warmth of her torso against his and the feel of her waist. His wriggling legs were his sole inspiration and the beat of his emotions marked the accent of his steps. It was the utmost pain and the greatest pleasure, greater still for being inconsequential. It was hell and heaven; hell for the abandonment of Miguel's emotions and heaven for the hope of redemption. But was Hellen meant to redeem him? She was just dancing; she was just taking what little free pleasure she could obtain from life. It was the perfect deal for her; nothing was demanded and nothing was taken away from her. It was pure existence, pure life and enjoyment; it was so feminine in essence: dancing to the beat of timelessness and placelessness; two spirits that rubbed each other to warm themselves up; nothing more than primary affection; nothing beyond furtive glances and erotic gestures which were meant to be food for future fantasies.

When the evening was over, the cycle of desire had been fulfilled for her. She'd felt coveted by a man; she'd seen her sexuality through his eyes and her beauty had been reassured for the time being. She didn't need him anymore. He, on the other hand, was burning with unfulfilled desire; the image of her solid thighs was imprinted on his mind. He couldn't wait to see her again.

Days passed, one after another, and Miguel collected a pile of unanswered messages and unimaginative excuses before resigning himself to the fact that she wasn't interested in him anymore.

## Chapter 4: You shall not steal

Miguel woke up with an overwhelming sensation of senselessness; the day before he had been cheated out of two thousand zloty by a stranger. The woman had left a message on a website asking for a loan for an urgent matter. Miguel had been enticed by it; he'd felt flattered by the idea of doing good to someone while earning some extra money in interest. Of course a thirty percent interest rate didn't look so extravagant to him. "There are people who live day by day," he thought, while he recalled many facts that proved it: his father's lack of capacity to put money away, a friend who had once explained to him his job as a money lender, as well as other friends who were inveterate gamblers and who worked a whole month for a salary that they'd spend in a few days. There was also the IMF's interest rate, as well as the adjustment measures taken to pay it, which had bankrupted his country. Everything led him to think that money was an immediate urgency for some people and that interest rates were as necessary as time is necessary for a tree to give fruits. But he'd mainly been deceived by the cleanness of the transaction. He didn't have to do anything but withdraw a bundle of printed paper and give it to someone who'd make good use of it. He'd only see some numbers less in his account; everything was so virtual, so dreamlike for him. The effortlessness of the action, the inertia that was started by his oral commitment to lend the money to the lady in need, were the facts that played the major role in setting the scene for his mistake.

Another intervening factor was his carelessness and impulsive behavior. Because at the beginning he had meant to go to the lady's house and demand documents from her. But his tight schedule didn't give him the chance to carry out his plan as intended, so he'd asked her to come to his university instead. At the moment when she appeared, he was going to make a copy of a contract he'd found online, which specified the terms of the deal. Everything looked in order; he'd taken all the measures to guarantee the success of the deal. But on his way he'd met a girl that shared a lecture with him. She was in an extrovert mood and they struck up a conversation. He checked the time a couple of times and after ten or fifteen minutes he thought it was too impolite of him to leave a desperate woman waiting. He came back to the lady and asked her to sign the contract. He asked to see her ID, but she said she'd forgotten; she'd brought an electricity bill instead. Miguel was apprehensive when he heard that, but then he looked at her. She must have been around thirty, but she looked aged with worries and work. She seemed so defenseless and distraught, and she looked at him with humbled dignity. He didn't want to believe that people could be brought to such extremes as to sell their souls for money. He trusted her out of idealism; he shut his eyes and hoped for her. He knew she was in tough straights; she'd told him her mother was ill and she needed the money for the rent. The prospect of getting his money back was not looking so solid at the time, but she promised to give it back, and he couldn't wait to finish the transaction so he could get back to pleasant affairs: talking with his classmate. The euphoria of talking with a nice girl can be comparable to the euphoria produced by alcohol, and Miguel was experiencing that feeling at the time. Everyone is careful not to drink before an important event, but no one is exempt from casual encounters that can alter our moods and make us underestimate our limitations. Miguel had been affected by this phenomenon and he'd overestimated his sensitiveness. He thought he could read the woman's spirit and he read in her look that she was an honest person. And probably she would've been, under other circumstances, under fairer conditions or if encouraged by more generous opportunities. But as it was, she was as righteous as she could be. In her current circumstances she'd been forced to deceive a stranger in order to get out of a mess, but it may have been just because she'd been too generous in a previous life and Miguel had taken too much from her, so much that now he needed to give some of it back.

This unfortunate event made him think about his future. He had some money left to finish his studies, but what about after that? He hadn't achieved anything career wise up to then and he didn't know where to start. He'd applied for everything, even jobs he didn't like, but without good results. But now that he'd lost half a month's salary he had an advantage: he didn't think so much about money. He'd rather get a job he knew he could keep for a long time, something in which he could excel. If he'd had some talent, he would've been a musician because he admired music above every other form of art. If he'd had the patience or the consistency, he would've been a scientist or a philosopher and would've discovered things that could help people. But he was neither talented nor patient enough; his only skill was to pour out disappointments on a blank page and do it with a little grace sometimes. The most precious gift nature had endowed him with was complexity of feelings and a never-ending capacity for introspection. There was nothing else he was really interested in other than speaking his mind to a virtual audience. He, like everyone else, wanted to be recognized for what he did, but, in contrast to others, who provide for real needs, he was just selling illusions that vanished as soon as the eyes were tired or the book was over. A person who steals your money is maybe doing you a favor in ridding you of your burden, but a person who steals your time and enthusiasm to fill you with delusions is unforgivable.

The act of forced charity that Miguel had performed might have been one of those chances life gives us to redeem ourselves. Miguel went to bed that night feeling a little relieved by the fact that he could plead mitigating circumstances when the time of his trial came.

## Chapter 5

It was five in the afternoon in Miguel's new apartment. He'd moved there because it was located in the city center and it was a good price for a nice room. He'd arranged all his stuff in a way that would be aesthetic but also practical. Fortunately, almost everything fit inside the wardrobe that came with the room. However, he had a few problems: two suitcases and a guitar that were too big to hide inside a wardrobe and a bunch of books of a considerable bulk. He slipped one suitcase underneath the wardrobe and put the other, handsomest, one against the wall. He left the guitar in a corner, covered with a plastic bag to prevent dust and humidity from damaging it.

He was going to have a party that day. It was the birthday of a pretty acquaintance named Luiza. He'd offered to cook for her so she could invite some friends over and celebrate the day. She'd promised to bring a cake and some sparkling beverage to make a toast at midnight. She had already repelled his advances, so he didn't want to invest too much emotionally in that party. However, he didn't exclude the possibility of her changing her mind about him, especially since she'd been sending him many messages of late. Furthermore, she'd hinted that, as it was a working day, they might be the only ones who'd stay till after midnight. He was dreaming of having that blue-eyed angel hanging around his bedroom.

She was objectively beautiful, if mere aesthetics were taken into account. She was not sexy, but she had subtle lines that denoted her femininity. She had small but well-shaped breasts that looked like rosebuds with a hint of full roses. She was rather short and her legs were thin, but she had good hips and her face was beautiful. Small greyish-blue eyes and a small red mouth delicately shaped. Besides, the whiteness of her skin set off her beautiful features. She seemed to enjoy Miguel's company and to want him around, and he thought that might lead to something. He was quieter than her in general, but she seemed to enjoy silence, in contrast to him, who got impatient when nothing was said. She spoke Polish to him and he was inwardly thankful for that; however, she seemed to want nothing from him and that worried him. He didn't mean to use her to learn the language; that wouldn't be honest or even productive. He was investing his time too, so he'd rather see some long-term results. However, he knew how it worked with girls; he knew that when he entered that misty world they inhabit, everything would be blurred and no possible goal would be clear. He'd have to play it cool, as his friend had told him. Hurrying would be no use so he'd have to go slow and steady, even when he didn't know where he was going. But, as he'd read in a yoga book: someone is lost only if he's looking for directions.

Things happened as expected, almost uneventfully. She played her role of the cold lady, but she did it with humanity. One of her friends came to the party quite late, which gave Miguel a reason for complaining. However, she asked Miguel in a sincere way if he minded her friend coming, which showed Miguel that she actually cared about his feelings. He was a little jealous, but just until her friend left and the party was over. They were left alone and he said: "Would you like to listen to some music?" To which she assented. Then it was just a matter of time until she got up and went to his room, which was the only place where they could listen to some music without disturbing his flat mates.

He happened to mention that the computer was in his room, as an implicit invitation for her to take the initiative towards more intimacy. She didn't react to the hint, but minutes later she stood up and walked like a hypnotized queen to his room. She was in control of the situation, or at least it seemed so to her. In any case, if superior forces aren't taken into account, she was surely in control. She entered the room and sat on the sofa automatically; the whole action was an assertion, a ceremonial act of taking possession of a newly acquired territory. He sat on the other corner of the sofa, sneaking his way nearer her. He laid the laptop on a bedside table and brought it closer to her, so she could pick the songs. She was domineering to the point of disliking virtually everything that he liked; that was her straightforward method of subjugation. He didn't mind; he seldom listened to music and her imposing her musical taste on him wasn't relevant at that moment. "Democracy is not so much about equality as it's about the division of tasks," he thought consolingly. She was the ruling class in this society, but he had the power of the mass, which is always conclusive.

She put on some songs, which were relegated to oblivion when they started talking. He tried to wrap his arm around her waist and get to kissing distance a couple of times, but she pulled back and stiffened every time, not without showering him with deprecatory remarks about his behavior. As if nothing had happened, she went on talking about her life until she touched upon religion. She was an assiduous churchgoer, not confining herself to Sundays for fulfilling her pious duty. He was bearing it all with glee until a cloud shadowed his mind.

"What's so eventful about Christ?" he said, "In which way does His life affect me?"

22

"If you believe that He died and was resurrected then there must be something to it, don't you think?" she answered.

"But I don't believe that."

"Then there's nothing else to be said about it; let's just listen to some good music."

But he wasn't content with that tacit agreement. Why was she so sure about her beliefs? He wanted to know what drew her to such religious fanaticism. He wanted to precipitate a resolution to his plight. He didn't want her avoiding a discussion with him; he wanted to define his position there and then.

"So that mean we can obviate the issue of God forever?" was the snare he used to bring back the subject.

"What issue of God?" she said, annoyed. "There's no issue about God. He exists, period. That you don't want to see it is the only issue in question." And thus she was caught in his dialectical trap. Now she'd shown her true colors. She was so sure of her position that every sign of disagreement from another person was considered a problem to be tackled patiently rather than another possible interpretation of reality.

"You're right; I don't want to see God. It's irrelevant to me." said Miguel. "Whether there's a God out there or not, I'm still responsible for my actions. And I personally believe that men re-created these insights we have of our nature and put them all down under a single god's name, as people put all responsibility on a king or lord. It's just a stratagem to homogenize faith; that's what it's all about. That's what Christianity has been all about from the beginning: homogenizing people's beliefs."

"Jeez, I can't believe my ears," answered Luiza. "How can you be so blind to the truth? How can men invent God? Are you out of your mind? How can we, limited creatures, create the eternal, the omnipotence, the omniscience? We can't even start to know God and you reason that men could have imagined something of that magnitude? It's just absurd to me."

"We are made in His image, aren't we?"

"Of course, but that doesn't mean that we enjoy His powers. We're mortals and our godly features are as transient as life."

"But we become eternal when we die, don't we?"

"Yes, either eternal bliss or eternal suffering, but we don't become God, if that's what you mean."

"We don't become God; we just return to His bosom, don't we?"

"Yes, we do, if we follow His commands on Earth."

"And how do we know what His commands are?"

"Are you making fun of me? We have the Bible, and then saints and enlightened people who showed us the way."

"So the Bible is the word of God, right? But it may have many interpretations, or it may not be applicable to my specific situation."

"The Bible is applicable to all situations. Everything is comprised there: present, future and past. You'll always find renewed hopes there."

"I believe that a believer may find hope in the Bible, but I don't believe it's applicable to everyone. I believe that saints set a good example, but people need to internalize the goodness or badness of each act; we can't follow patterns if we want to live a real life."

"And what's a real life for you? A life of transgression and chaos? You prefer fulfilling your egotistic desires, satiating your low instincts rather than following God's orders? If you choose to disobey your Father who loves you, you're condemning yourself and society."

"So it's a simple matter of obedience then? Be a good boy and you'll earn heaven; be bad and you'll be punished. Does God work as society does, with reward and punishment?"

"God Works His will through divine order. He doesn't punish you. He just gives you your just deserts for your deeds."

"The same as society, I guess. If I steal, then what do I deserve?"

"You'll go to hell if you don't repent."

"So is stealing good or bad?"

"Stealing is wrong; God and society condemn it."

He'd proved his point to himself. The conviction with which she held her beliefs didn't come from any personal revelation, but from the pressure of a society that molds the system in which people live. He was a little taken aback by this insight, but he dared to say: "So society has the same power to condemn as God has?"

"A Christian society, built in God's image, surely has. We need to condemn evil, not to consent to it with our silence. That's our duty as Christians: to denounce evil on earth."

Miguel had heard enough for a day and he didn't want to go on with a cyclical discussion. He wanted to conclude the subject in one way or another. "I agree that we need to denounce evil, but I don't agree that someone holds the only key to the distinction between good and evil. Every one of us needs to decide that, and that's the difference between our religious and moral beliefs and the laws of society."

"There's no truth outside God. Dark is the path of those who choose to walk without Him."

"I know, I know." He said, in a final effort to agree with her, and the subject was dropped. She smiled a complacent smile and sat back, reassured on her dogmatic throne, while he felt he'd grown tremendously out of the exchange of ideas and beliefs between them. He saw the points in common and the places of discordance. He saw the way to agree with her and the point till which he could go along with her until their paths were divided. He hoped that they would never reach that point.

*The call of the heart is low-pitched and rhythmical,*
*beating steadily through the sprees of life,*
*we can hum all the tunes we fancy,*
*but our heart will never miss a beat.*
*Dancing to the rhythm instead of the melody,*
*we can have a silence and there'll still be music*
*to our ears in unison with our feet that know*

*to step on the beat, dancing through life's festival.*

*Follow no road but that of your self-enjoyment,*
*carry no resentment, but go on light-heartedly,*
*no boundaries to trespass as we tread our paths,*
*no landmarks, no ruins of foregone fair sights,*
*the goal is not ahead, but always beside you,*
*when there's nothing to see, it's time to move on,*
*new veins and hues of leaves stimulating the eye,*
*and tiredness is diffused in the boundless greenery.*

*Happiness is staying up to recover some sleep tomorrow,*
*It's having something to worry about,*
*and fearing to lose it,*
*It's knowing it can go away anytime, any moment,*
*as simply as it came,*
*it's hope that if it ends, new happiness will always come*
*to stay with me, make me some company*
*on this lonely path,*
*happiness is today without tomorrow.*

*About revolutions and hats that change in fashion and color*
*and look good on us, and our struggle to start*
*each day with a new emotion, grabbing this or that one*
*to parade it on our heads, and my ever spanning*
*the gap between us with verses that revolt and change color*
*and fashion and I wear them each day and every time*
*that I feel alien to you, and I'm more myself but you*
*read my verses and stifle a revolution and a hat*
*pleases you and you snap it from me and you wear it.*

## Chapter 6

Miguel always traveled by tram. It was the most efficient means of transport in a medium- sized city like Poznan. He was fascinated by the frequency of the stops; there was one every two hundred meters sometimes. This gave him the impression of a carousel traversing the town, which you could get on and off more for fun than for real need. The trams were efficient enough, but the buses were subjected to the vicissitudes of traffic; besides, taking a bus wasn't so much fun. Those colorful worms wriggled their way through the middle of the streets, with their electric antennas sparkling on rainy days. Those metallic annelids with silent feet ambushed people on the crosswalks and stalked cars on their way to work. Miguel felt the empowering sensation of boarding the tram; the only case of boarding in which no slopes were involved. He could surf uphill as well as downhill and he didn't have the luxury of being able to stretch his arms to get a better balance, but he needed to surf among people hanging from elastic bands or attached to the back of the seats. There were all kinds of people on trams: hurried people, whose forced inaction gave them an air of despair and wildness; dreamy people, whose absentmindedness was a shield against the life pulsing around them; ponytailed guys: those recalcitrant goths and gaels sitting peacefully beside octogenarian ladies. There were also short-haired young women, who seemed to be the sequel of the feminist movement and the subsequent obliteration of gender roles; "They have taken away from us the high heels and leading positions at work; we should claim the lipstick and the ability to cry on command," thought Miguel.

Miguel had entered the tram through the back and had made his way to an empty seat beside a handsome girl. She was busy with her recollections of days from the recent past, but he could feel her tacit warming welcoming; she made space by taking her handbag from the seat and putting it on her lap and she even sat straighter than before, as a sign of deference towards the newcomer. He couldn't help casting a few glances at her profile, which, to his relief, was rather plain, but he didn't notice any reaction on her part. After a few minutes, she stared at him for a few seconds and he, aware of the situation, did what his instincts told him: he looked her in the eye. Her light blue eyes were as he had expected, heavenly, and he couldn't help feeling delightful satisfaction at having accomplished his mission: a first class contact with the wild sex, deservedly known as the fair sex. She smiled a knowing smile at him as he delayed his automatic reaction a second or two. His eyes, which seconds before had been focused on a book in his hands, were vacant as if he were coming back from a reverie. He feigned ignorance of the ruling norms of social transport and for a second he made believe that they had just clicked on a tram, for no further reason than mutual attraction. But he dropped the game lest she miss her stop, and he made space for her to pass by him and get off the tram.

Miguel's day was meant to be jovial, but that day he had a meeting with Luiza or, as he was fond of calling her, the religious girl. A common acquaintance had introduced them, and at the beginning he thought that some of the appreciation and interest his acquaintance had for him had been transferred to Luiza and that had helped make him dearer in her eyes. But now he wasn't so sure about that because Luiza seemed to have reasons of her own to be interested in him.

The conversation during most of the meeting was centered on Luiza; she liked talking about herself and Miguel was the perfect listener, as he seldom had something to say. He left her at her door and walked back home. He liked her and she was nice to him; she had just been too overwhelmed with her problems that day, so her sensitivity had been impaired. She'd said a couple of things that had hurt his pride before, but on this occasion she had overbalanced him emotionally. The thing she said that hurt his pride was that he should meet other girls. She had noticed his emotional involvement and she gave him this advice. He couldn't accept the fact of her not being jealous of him after they'd spent so much time together. That demoralized him because he didn't want to waste all the effort he'd spent on her. The only reason he was still around her was because he still held some hopes that she'd fall in love with him. However, she didn't miss a chance to reassure him of the opposite and she even playfully provoked him to meet other girls.

But that day she said something that had worse consequences for him because it actually had an effect on his actions. He was looking for work and he'd applied for some jobs in other cities too. He preferred to stay in Poznan, but he'd never seriously considered the fact of moving out. However, now he had a serious decision to make: whether he'd take a job in another city or not. There was no formal reason for him to stay, except for the fact that he still expected good things to happen to him there. He was telling Luiza about the situation when she said: "But up to when are you staying here? Because if you're going to Warsaw, then I need to take the things I left at your place."

Those words gave him the impression that she felt that their relationship was a transient one. She wasn't counting on him for her future, so it was natural for her to consider their being apart, but the fact that this was a matter of fact for her gave him a shock of reality. He was nothing special for her; he wasn't indispensable in her life. In his moment of indecision, he needed something more than that to stay; he needed her to claim him and not to evince that she'd easily let him go.

"I may also move out of this city; I'm fed up with it," she said. "I've had enough; I'll go somewhere else, where nobody knows me."

"But why do you want to leave everything you have?" he asked.

"I just want to leave and start all anew," was her answer.

He knew that feeling because he'd also done the same, and that was what scared him: the reality of her assertion. He couldn't allow himself to stay for a girl who wasn't interested in him. The first thing you know she could have gathered her things and gone where the wind blows. There was no way for him to influence her decision; he felt inane, futile and meaningless for her. And he felt that meaninglessness affecting his own life. But she was so meaningful to him and that was what was most important. If she didn't need him, he'd go away with a light consciousness and start all anew also. He knew it was useless to get attached, but he couldn't see all his possibilities because he was acting on wishful thinking rather than facts. He desired things to happen to him rather than giving them the chance to actually happen. He was trying to force something that should be as natural as two desires combining into a single goal. He was just tarrying, waiting hopefully for some satisfaction of his needs, but he didn't know up to what point he would be able to keep that unstable situation going on.

They walked through the parks that were strewn across the city. The night was pitch dark and the dim light of the lamps filled the air with a dreary sensation that was mingled with the inherent gloominess of their conversation. However, those two lonely people were kindred; those individual souls found relief from their daily burden in the communion of their sorrows.

Their following meeting took place in a more hopeful environment; he'd just opened a window of her apartment because he'd felt stifled by the heat of the room, when she told him something that shed more light on the situation. She was brokenhearted because of her previous experiences and she couldn't see any hopes for her professional future. He couldn't empathize with her; he rather despised her for having such a vulgar tendency to live in the past and worry about the future. He started seeing her as a hungry lion roaring her discontent away. He knew it was impossible for him to blame his discontentment on someone or something in particular. "In general I'm too melancholic to give a damn about people and the world" he told her, "let alone get depressed because of them." She just listened to him, puckering her lips and showing no intention to breach the gap between their different approaches to life. She just got up to close the window because, after all, "autumn has already started," she said, "and I'm sure you don't want to catch a cold."

He waited for her to finish whatever she was doing and saying about windows and cold, which, to his mind, were mere distraction tricks to which she resorted to try to avoid confrontation with reality. He told her that the only remnants of primitive desire he had left were his passion for girls and writing; everything else was indifferent to him. His economic and professional situation wasn't more flattering than hers, he told her, and nevertheless, "you're making such a big deal of it." She just rolled her eyes and sighed deeply. She knew she was giving too much importance to her problems, but after all, those were her problems and she felt she had the right to do with them as she pleased.

In reality, he despised her for having rejected him, for denying him a chance to make her happy even when she was drowning in loneliness. It hurt his pride to hear her talk of her unhappiness, for she'd chosen that unhappiness rather than being with him. He was angry at her for suffering from unfulfilled desires and great expectations. He wanted just her and she wanted so many things; he needed just her willingness to be happy, and there she was: suffering from something alien to him. And what was a career or success to him? What did it matter which city he lived in or what he did for a living? He felt he would've given it all up for her; he had that feeling already rooted in his heart.

She understood his anxiety, but she couldn't check her anxiety and appease her fears. She was telling him all that so there would be no ghosts between them; so he'd know all the dark areas of her spirit and he would never be afraid of her. She wanted to explain to him what her situation was all about; she argued that he didn't understand her because he'd never been through something similar. He agreed with her that he'd never been in a similar situation because he'd never climbed up too high so he couldn't fall too low. He was on a step from which success and depression were totally out of reach. However, he hated her for the peak of excitement she wanted to reach; that summit she looked up to and which

31

she was so far from reaching. If she could just look around her, content herself and be happy, but, "...and this is something I know from experience," he told her, "no one can force you to be happy."

She assented with her head, in a submissive gesture that meant that she agreed, but she couldn't help feeling what she felt. She just hoped all his emotions would last long enough to lead somewhere. She'd grown fond of his tantrums and outbursts of passion; they reminded her of the life full of excitement and joy which she had fancied so many times. She didn't want to give him vain hopes and she wasn't sure of anything in her life. She felt sorry for herself and guilty for making him suffer like that. However, he did seem to enjoy her company and that gave her hope. She hoped that their meetings meant as much to him as they meant to her.

For Miguel it was different. He was in an impasse now because she was seeking his company, but he couldn't get as close as he wished. This tantalizing situation unnerved him because the normal emotional strength everyone needs to get detached from someone who does not answer to their needs was neutralized by her appealing to him for support. He felt more strongly than ever the absurdity of life in her behavior towards him. He imagined her as an elephant looking for something she was trampling on; he knew she couldn't help it, but he didn't want to be part of it.

He wanted the sweetest revenge of all; he wanted her to become dependent on him to the point of not being able to imagine life without him. He knew he was deluding himself, but he saw no way out but to be as selfless as possible, to love her to the point in which all desire for her would die and just pity would remain. Then, when she desired him, he'd have his revenge because he'd already be over her. But what for all this drama? Even if he succeeded, he'd get nothing positive out of her, just negative pleasure. He still had to find a girl who requited his love, someone he could build a life with. "Why not focus on positive feelings rather than tarrying in hatred?" He thought. "Wouldn't it be as good a revenge to leave her to deal with her situation alone?" It would even be more practical for him and morally constructive for her. That's what he'd do; his mind was made up. However, as usual, his emotions didn't follow suit.

*Every day brings anew the sun*
*and every morning, new surprises.*
*Yesterday I left you walking on the shore*
*of that sea we discovered together.*
*Yet you aren't lonely, my hope*
*reaches out to you and fills*
*your every step with meaning.*
*Wherever you go, no wonder*
*you can listen to my song*
*that sings to your health*
*and mine, as I claim*
*a share in your happiness.*

*Leaning my thoughts into the Polish afternoon,*
*I found you smiling at my effect on you,*
*and your eyes sparkle with eventualities*
*that you've derived from the way I stare at you.*
*Then you look away and I glance around me,*
*the chain of events has suddenly been broken,*
*other stories are built, subplots in our story,*
*which may be as long as our wishfulness.*
*You lean your own thoughts into the afternoon*
*and read our story with enchanted eyes,*
*the theme is of your taste, the plot pleases you*
*and you add a page more to be written.*

*You don't sleep I don't sleep,*
*the tacit stars, warm night of April,*
*glazed dancing eyes that spoke in reveries*
*about you, your modern ways,*
*the manners in which you're different*
*but so oppressively similar*
*to some modernist thought*
*I once had about you.*

*With dolls in her eyes,   around my torso she twined*
*her impassive allure.   Satiated to disdain*
*I donned without pain     her relish so pure.*
*For her to step around      a playground of mute songs,*
*her eyes fixed on dolls    impassively playing,*
*I'll recreate the beauty    that wanders towards dolls*
*among my silent songs      on our playground laying.*

*Don't break the spell of life*
*as a mock-up of pasteboard.*
*I set the pieces,*
*you scrutinize them,*
*I color them, you like them,*
*we build a heaven all anew.*
*Then we leave it to go*
*and toil on earth.*

## Chapter 7

Steven had called Miguel unexpectedly; he always did. He wanted him to
meet him an hour before an important World Cup match. They met at a
shopping mall and Steven proposed they go to sit somewhere quiet. They
made casual conversation while Steven ate a big hamburger; he said he

was so busy he hadn't had time to eat before. After having finished his meal and taken some sips from his coke, he pulled out his Bible. He said he wanted to share a passage with Miguel, to which Miguel assented. It was a famous passage, which they read until the part that says: "For God did not send the Son into the world to judge the world, but that the world might be saved through Him."

He asked him what he thought about it and Miguel gave some vague answers about the symbolic meaning of the snake in the stick and the beauty of the metaphor of life's spirit as the wind, which no one knows where it comes from or where it goes. Steven started explaining the passage in detail, denoting background knowledge in the matter. He asked Miguel what he thought about it all and Miguel answered that it was really poetical. Steven asked whether he felt the Kingdom of God coming to him through those words; whether he felt Jesus in his heart. Miguel answered that he wasn't a Christian because he didn't believe in Jesus as God, but he did believe those were inspired words.

"So tell me what you believe in then," said Steven. "Do you believe in a god?"

"Yes, I do," answered Miguel, "but it's not a god that you can call Father or Master; it's all of us and each of us."

"So how do you explain evil? Why do evil things happen?" Where does it come from?"

"I don't believe in evil. Sin is just an error caused by lack of contemplation."

"So who decides what is a sin and what isn't? Who judges us?"

"No one judges us; it's just cause and effect. We do something and we get the results."

"And who created the universe?"

"Nothing created the universe. The universe came from nothing."

"How can something come from nothing? Have you ever seen that happen in nature?"

"You haven't seen God either and you believe He woke up one day and decided to play builder's yard for seven days. But the truth is that it's a mystery and I'm just conjecturing to make you happy. The only thing I'm sure of is that I don't know. The passage you read also says that no one has been to heaven and come back and that's the most important part. No one really knows what's up there."

"So you'd rather believe that we all came from nothing? How can this be more plausible than a superior force taking care of all this?"

"Imagine light and darkness. Darkness is defined as the lack of light, but that's not a good definition because darkness makes light possible. Darkness is the place where light comes to be; it isn't just an entity in itself, but it's ontologically superior to light because it exists without light. That's God, our creator: pure darkness."

"God is darkness? He's nothing? Again I ask you, how can this darkness and nothingness bring light and beauty to life?"

"In the same way as the stars that exist far away whose light we can't see yet. They exist potentially for us and it was the same in the beginning. We existed potentially, latently, as everything in the world. If you believe in God's plan, then you know about it. We were meant to be; we were word or thought before our physical manifestation. We just don't need to bring another being into the equation; otherwise we'll be trapped in a never-ending creationist chain. Because if God is eternal and omnipresent, He can only be emptiness and darkness: these things exist everywhere and predate everything. So then nihilists aren't so mistaken when they believe there's nothing. Their only mistake is that this assertion carries a negative connotation for them. To say there's nothing does not mean that everything is lacking but rather that everything's full of nothingness. And anyway, this does not affect us morally, as we still have the cause-and-effect law to govern us, whether our nature is light or darkness."

Steven told Miguel that he needed to leave; the match between Brazil and Germany was going to start. Miguel wondered what could lead an

American to be interested in football and spirituality; those two things seemed alien to the American culture. He walked back home hoping for Brazil to win the match so Argentina could have their dream final: winning against Brazil in their own country.

## Chapter 8

The German football team was sitting together in the hall of their third-world hotel, overlooking the favelas. It was one of the most expensive hotels in town, but some people had complained about the occasional gunshots awakening them in the middle of the night. However, the German team slept to the sound of cascades, which were deliberately played during the whole night in order to muffle any furtive gunshots. They were having their usual cola and hamburger feast as they did on every special occasion. In general they were under a strict regime of protein and vitamins, with extra amounts of iron and magnesium before and after a game, but today they were chilling out; they had won their match already and, like ancient Greek warriors after a battle, they were celebrating their triumph by indulging their appetites. This was an instinct as deeply rooted in them as in ancient Greeks, and the coach, who knew about it, allowed them a big hamburger and a big glass of coke to appease this immemorial beast. Be that as it may, the German team was watching TV and gulping hamburgers in the middle of a World Cup which they still were part of.

-Where is Arnold? He's missing the match.

-He must have gone to see the girls from the samba team; they've been parading their bodies around since they learnt we were staying here.

-Yes, they are a bunch of attractive girls. I'd like to get hold of one for half-an-hour. If only the coach didn't have such strict rules, we could be having the time of our lives instead of getting bored with this game.

-How can you possibly get bored with such a game? It's really tight and Brazil may get out.

-Yes, just focus on the man you'll mark; he's gonna give you a headache if they win the match.

-That son of a Brazilian bitch is gonna leave a small gap and it'll be their ruin; you'll see.

-I'm glad you're so confident. Actually, I think we can easily break their defense; it doesn't look well-organized.

-Yes, and what are they doing at the front? They seem not to want to score. I hate this South American melodrama; why don't they score and stop giving hopes to their poor rivals?

-Not everyone has your cold blood in front of the goal, Dale; you should have a little consideration towards the less gifted.

-Funny, funny, but what you say is true; I'm a coldblooded hound and you throw me a ball and I'll put it where it must be: at the back of the net.

-But look! He seems to be injured.

-Yes, he's wriggling with pain. The son of a bitch hit him on the lower back.

-He's not getting up. He'll be taken off on a stretcher.

-Here's a man who won't play for a while.

-Without him in their team, we're sure to win against them.

-Yes, it won't even be fun and everyone will pity them for having lost their star. I hate this commercial sport sometimes.

-We'll defeat them so badly that there won't be a single doubt that we would've won the match anyway.

-So that's the plan then? It sounds quite easy to me.

-Yes, let's just wait for a few minutes more; maybe they'll be knocked out today anyway.

-Yes, in that case I'll just go home and you guys can stay. You can win this World Cup without me and with your eyes closed.

The following Wednesday Germany played Brazil in the Minerao Stadium. Brazil was still bleeding from the wound and the Germans saw the chance and attacked relentlessly. One after another, the balls landed in the back of the goal like oranges land in a housewife's shopping basket. Germany showed no respect for the grandfather of football, the country with more experience in World Cups and a worthy rival for anyone under any circumstances. For Germany, it was now and here. There was nothing sacred or even eventful about playing Brazil; they played them as they would've played Iran or England. In any case, it made no difference who they played against; the only thing they thought about was winning; other things were totally irrelevant. Whenever they could beat their opponents, they did; whenever they lost, they just lowered their heads and waited until a new opportunity for victory presented itself. It was a simple business for them; they knew the twists and turns of the game and did not take it personally if they lost or won. Like a bloodthirsty lion strolling the grassland of the Serengeti, they kept their sedate demeanor until prey happened to fall into their clutches. They had shown the madness of their killing rage in this match; they had torn their prey to pieces out of pure instinct. A dead animal couldn't be deader, but the sight of the blood aroused primeval feelings in them, and thus they kept senselessly battering the corpse of a worthy rival until they made it unworthy by force of humiliation. Now they were in the finals, lying in wait for their next victim.

Meanwhile Brazil was a boiling pot. Brazilians had demonstrated against the high expenditure on the World Cup and now that their team had lost, they were simply outraged. With rampant crime and poverty in the streets and without the comfort of being the best football players in the world, all in addition to the fact of having been humbled in their own country, the Brazilian crowd grew more restless every day. Rumor had it that if Brazil lost the match for third place against Holland, the popular discontentment would be so great that the finals would have to be cancelled. And they did lose, but nothing of that sort happened. Brazilians, though passionate, are good losers; they've been through every World Cup and, although they've won quite a few of them, they've tasted the gall of defeat. They just bowed their heads and stoically accepted a second defeat; enough tears had already been shed in the previous match.

The second team to make it to the finals was Argentina; they had played miserly during the whole World Cup, always winning by the smallest difference or penalties. However, the Argentinian team had an aura of tragic heroism; they respected every team they took on and played as if their lives depended on it. It was such a dramatic way of playing that Argentinians thanked God euphorically for every match they won and they couldn't believe it when they reached the semi-finals. Behind them there weren't the spoils of vanquished opponents but the milestones of a fierce struggle to victory. Argentina had been previously humbled by Germany so that wasn't something they feared anymore. They could accept the idea of losing and winning would be just another reason to think that God is Argentinian. The only thing they needed to do was to step onto the field and hope the longing in their hearts would make their legs run; the rest was in a superior force's hands. They had their own hero too: the smallest and trickiest player of all times, excluding Maradona. They'd relied on him to win their matches, but he hadn't excelled as his international fans expected. What international fans don't know is that football is a team sport and that all the efforts of rival teams to neutralize the hero were detrimental to their overall defense and as a result other Argentinian players had an easier path to the goal.

The finals took place in the Maracana Stadium. Most of the prognostics had been favorable to Germany before the World Cup started and now most football fans supported them because of their sweeping victories. People like winners and most Europeans took the side of their local heroes; however, there were some Italians and Spaniards still supporting Argentina; in the end this would prove to be a bad idea. Argentina did the best they could, but it wasn't enough to grant them a world title. They adjusted their defense so as not to run any risks, which made for a first half dominated by Germany. They had the control of the ball in the second half, but as the match ended in a draw, they went to extra time. The match was tight and anyone could have won, but, as luck always has it, Argentina was fated to be the protagonist of a tragedy. In the last eight minutes, Germany scored the goal that sealed their victory and Argentina saw their first final in twenty-four years slip from their hands. Again Germany, that cursed adversary, was going to take the title away from them. The Argentinian team, used to tragedies, just bowed their heads and went back home, which fortunately wasn't so far away.

## Chapter 9

*Elle travailla pour vivre ; puis, toujours pour vivre, car le coeur a sa faim aussi, elle aima.-* Les Misérables.

"I've just sent a conclusive message to Luiza," said Miguel to Leo. "I've told her that I'm tired of the situation and I'd prefer not to see her so often, that I don't want to be her friend and that she'd better look for someone who's disinterestedly friendly."

"OK, do what feels right."

"Of course, man, I'm human. I'll go out with some other girl; I can't have unsolved mysteries in my head. Whatever she wants from me, let it wait till our next life together."

Miguel had met Luiza's parents. For no apparent reason, she'd invited him to meet them and Miguel was unsettled about it. He knew it was supposed to mean she cared about him, but he didn't see it in her attitude towards him. He felt that Luiza was too sly for him to make out. He felt she was continually teasing him, leading him to believe that there was something between them. He didn't know if she did it on purpose or out of the blind female instinct for sadism. She didn't seem to have any need for him and all of her invitations were so casual that he didn't know whether to feel encouraged or discouraged by them. But why did she want to see him so frequently then? She'd already said she wasn't interested, so theoretically she was just killing time with him. She looked too kindhearted for that kind of behavior, but he'd been disappointed many times and he'd learned to see potential evils even in the nicest people. Of course, she wasn't aware of it, but she was harming him; it wasn't even her obligation to take care of his feelings or to calculate all the consequences of her actions. Miguel knew that everyone is master of their own lives and this anguished him because it was up to him either to speak out or simply draw apart from her.

He'd met her parents expecting to get closer to her, but she still didn't show signs of interest. He knew there are no magic formulas for love, but it was in his romantic nature to expect the impossible. When he was walking her back home, he realized that the evening had been inconsequential to their lives, that everything would go back to its regular course and that they were going to be still mere friends. He couldn't stem a flood of melancholy that lasted for a couple of days. Whenever they met after that, he wouldn't look at her but at a distant horizon, which seemed as far away as his hopes of ever being with her. He hadn't kept meeting her just because of lack of willpower; it was rather his latent hope of their being together. His relationship with her reminded him of his first ideas of romance, in which everything was platonic and the effect of a single smile could last him for weeks. When he'd started romancing he was a melancholic guy and everything was tinged by his mood, even his ideas of love. So the most romantic scene for him was one in which two people mutually confessed their fears and bitterness and then cried on each other's shoulders. Later on he'd heard that good humor is the key to a woman's heart and he'd successfully adopted a more lighthearted attitude towards relationships with women, but he'd always kept his primitive idea of love intact. He felt a latent passion for the first time in a long while and he would renounce his desire to be with her forever just for the pleasure of being with her now.

*There was the emotional terrorism of good lovers between them.*

Luiza had started to acclimatize herself to Miguel. She didn't acknowledge that she needed him, but she showed signs of attachment and possessiveness. After she'd received a discouraging message from him in which he said he didn't want to see her again, she reacted in the most unexpected way: she looked for him. It was the night of the football match between Germany and Argentina, and Miguel had planned to watch it on a big screen set up outdoors at a café especially for the occasion. She arrived there before him and waited for him in a chair, without talking to anyone or mingling with the crowd. She'd expected to find some familiar faces, but none of Miguel's acquaintances were there. She didn't know what posture to assume when he arrived; she was at fault because she hadn't been invited by him; she'd tried to be independent and have fun in spite of the message she'd received, which she deemed rude and uncalled-for; she wanted to show him that he'd made a huge mistake, but she failed. Just from his look she could tell that she looked sad to him, that he was going to approach her out of pity because he was considerate and not because he really wanted to. She accepted his generosity like a beggar who accepts the few coins a gentleman puts in his hand. She'd already humbled herself by going there; she couldn't change that, but she could try not to tacitly ask for more than what he'd already given her. She'd planned to behave in such a self-sufficient way in front of him that he'd think that she went there just to see how he was doing, maybe out of worry at his strange message. If he asked, she'd say that she wanted to make sure he didn't get upset if his team lost the match. There were many excuses for her to be there and she didn't want to think of the fact that she was there simply and definitely because she couldn't be without him. The fact that the match went wrong had no great influence on Miguel's mood; however, it set the tone for a philosophical mood that made him think of what he had and what he didn't. Luiza was something he didn't have; she was there, but she could just as easily have been doing something somewhere else. He knew she'd never watched football before, her lack of knowledge about it gave away this fact, but he didn't know that she was there for him. In his view, her reasons for being there could vary from simply being free that night to not wanting to change her mind after having already planned to go there. He felt responsible for her presence there; after all he'd mentioned the event to her and had indirectly invited her. But what was she doing there after he'd clearly expressed his wish not to see her?

He saw she was alone and in her eyes he saw the pain of hurt pride; he went up to her and tried to seem as glad as possible about her having come. Actually, he was happy to see her, he always was, but it was upsetting to know that he didn't have control over his emotions and that her mere presence could draw him to her. His plan to get detached from her had failed, or maybe not; maybe it had succeeded. Now she was there uninvited, it was her own fault; everything he did was going to be out of his good-heartedness, and that was a fact. He sat beside her and introduced her to an acquaintance of his so she could talk to someone. However, he didn't monopolize her company; he left her alone after he saw her exchange some words with a guy. He sat beside her, but talked to other girls and people around him.

When the match was over and he left without saying goodbye, Luiza felt a sting of solitude in her spine. She'd drunk a beer and she wasn't used to drink; the effect of the alcohol was combined with her sudden sadness and she felt she was falling off a precipice. She texted him asking if he was well, but she actually meant to ask if everything was well between them. He answered her that it was just sports and that he was fine, which didn't soothe her. She hadn't asked the right question and had received an unsatisfactory answer. She let the warm drops of a warm shower wash her unhappiness away and then tried to sleep. She shut her eyes tightly and this extra effort she put into sleeping was the cause of her staying awake the whole night. She slept the whole morning and at noon, when she got up, the new day struck her as monotonous and senseless. She was so blue that she couldn't do anything except trying to gain back Miguel's good regard for her. It was her only goal for that day and she'd feel satisfied if she could do at least that. She'd cook something for him and be as nice as possible. She'd efface herself and do whatever he wanted for an afternoon; she'd try to please him in every possible aspect. She texted him and he accepted her invitation to dinner. They ate and shared the whole afternoon together and the ties that bound them grew stronger, and her mood grew lighter and calmer.

A few days after that episode, she felt confident enough to invite him to a group meeting that was very important for her, a religious meeting organized in a church. She unconsciously wanted him to have the same beliefs as her and to defend the same values. Those meetings were stimulating for her and she thought it might be interesting for him too. However, the meeting was a failure and Miguel was bored to death. She couldn't explain enough that the previous meeting had been much more interesting and that she'd also got bored this time; Miguel was deaf to reason. They walked back home with some people from the religious group and found a homeless man on the street. He had something written on a board and it was supposed to be funny and to attract people, but Miguel didn't notice it. However, a guy from the group approached the man and started talking to him while he threw some coins into a can he had in front of him. The man told them that his wife had wronged him and that he had two children back in his village. He also used to have a house and a car and he had a degree in psychology, but after what he'd been through, he decided to leave his village and travel in search of a cure for his heartbreak. He said he was tired of begging and there were people who insensitively told him to get a job and stop bothering them in the street. He was fed up with his situation and he hoped to get a job in the following days, although not a well-paid one. When they asked him where he slept and what he ate, he said that he managed and he didn't go further into that subject; it really seemed like he was paying a self-inflicted penitence there in the street and that he wasn't looking for economic relief but spiritual redemption. All this astonished Miguel, who cursed those religious people's good luck; they'd found the only beggar that didn't want money but comprehension and kind words. They prayed for him in the middle of the street and they were well-satisfied with their daily good deed. All this was compelling for Miguel, who didn't believe in coincidences; he would've kept going to their meetings were it not for the fact that they were so boring. That was one of the most important rules of his life: to avoid numbing himself in any way, whether by drinking too much alcohol or by taking up senseless activities. The only thing left for him to do was to acknowledge that these people came in handy sometimes and that they did help people sometimes. He'd always respected or felt intrigued by religious people, but now he admired how in tune they were with life. They seemed to be more sensitive to other's suffering; however, he didn't know if this came from their religious learning or from the fact that most of them had suffered a lot themselves. When the group split up it was already late. Miguel could only think of home at that time and he said that to Luiza, although they'd planned to go to another meeting. She bade him goodnight and said that she'd go by herself for an hour and he exploded. He was upset at her self-sufficient attitude, but he was more upset because he'd had to bear that awful meeting till the end, all because of her, and now he wasn't in the mood to stay out any longer. He thought of her as a selfish creature who only wants to have a good time and go to sleep in a good mood. He told her she could go alone, but that she'd better not invite him to do anything after that. She listened to him impassively, but ended up yielding to his desires. At first it was hard for her to understand what ailed him, but when she understood, she generously offered to do what he wanted. He wanted to be alone with her, not to share her with others. They went for a walk around the decrepitly dark city. He learned that he was the reason for her low mood the day after the match. It was a revelation to him, who up to then had thought that she wasn't interested in him at all. She told him she was sad because he'd left without saying goodbye to her and she'd felt abandoned. Miguel appreciated her courage and her finally opening herself up to him. However, he was still hurt from the last time she'd rejected him; he knew she was capable of harming him so he didn't have any pity for her. He walked her home and the next morning he wrote to her:

*I don't want you to misunderstand my opinion, in case it's important to you. Yesterday's group was interesting, especially the girl who bravely told the story of her life. The priest is friendly and I liked it when we stopped in front of that man; for me it is always important to know there are people who are in a worse situation than us. The fact that he is educated and has been through a difficult situation, but still believes in life is inspiring to me. So I like your friends and I think they're good company for you. This environment is a little too religious for me, and I was as bored as you'd be watching science fiction with me. That's all. I hope you had a good night.*

## Chapter 10

Miguel was thinking of his past life in Argentina. Everything came to him vividly, as in a touristic journey with hours of leisure to enjoy the scenery. He could see the palm trees in the distance and the sun overwhelmingly present over the whole place. There were national roads traversing villages and getting you to innumerable cities. You needed only to follow the asphalt, to veer in some direction and in a few hours you were sure to end up traversing the main street of a big city or the outskirts of a small village until you finally lost your identity among cabins, desolate parks, tire shops and scattered gas stations. In the end you could get to some government building painted in orangish pink and know that you were in the city center. Then you just had to take the broadest street in view and go straight the whole way until you found a new road that would take you somewhere else.

New roads meant new destinies and Miguel knew he didn't need any passport to change climate and landscape; he was in the Argentinean Union, which had once been meant to be a unitary state, like most of the countries in the world, but which had finally opted for a federation. Like in the European Union, all the member states enjoyed the privilege of traveling without a visa inside the confines of the Argentinian Area and also had a common currency: the Peso. Outside the Union were potential world empires like Brazil and better organized countries, like Uruguay, which a long time ago had gently declined to join the budding federation of states, and Chile, which had recently defended its control over the Beagle Chanel from Argentina's claims. There was also Paraguay, an ex-member state, from which a piece of land had been taken as retaliation for an expansive impulse led by one of its strongmen in 1864.

It was too hot and he wanted some glacial cold for a change. He just had to head south and that wasn't too difficult to do during the day: he just had to drive away from the noon sun. During the night, he needed only to follow the Southern Cross. He decided to take the former option as there was still daylight. He drove for miles on end dodging the occasional suicidal cows that cut across his path in a most parsimonious manner. These cows came from nowhere and everywhere; people just bump into them on their way to their cottages, while walking through meadows and grassland, climbing over barbwire or crossing fluvial canals. Sometimes they club them on the head if they happen to have a suitable piece of wood nearby. Near the kill they light a carefully confined fire so the smoke would guide them when they came back with a cart. They have a butcher's knife and maybe a saw to cut up the carcass so they can carry it home. Some other cows just appear at people's doors and demand food in an ignominious way that remind them of stray dogs and hobos that haven't learned good manners. So after they've thrown them the leftovers of their lunch, they might pen them up and fatten them to have good milk, daily breaded cutlets and a good weekly piece of roast beef, which the locals call 'azado.' The pasta to accompany this delicacy isn't so easy to get;

48

people need to grow their own wheat and pay someone of Italian descent to transform it magically into spaghetti and other varieties of noodles. Miguel drove for fifteen hours on a road that got lost on the horizon. The sun was always behind him, but eventually it flared into a flamboyant sunset and night fell. It was still hot and in addition to that he was hungry and sleepy. He was in the middle of some slum and people were offering him big roasted sausages called 'chorizos.' "Everything is roasted in this country," thought Miguel, while he served himself some ketchup and mustard from the counter. "I'm thirstier than ever," he thought. "These people really know how to do business." He also bought a beer that by chance happened to be offered at the same street stall. He couldn't believe that a grill and a fridge could get along convivially in the middle of the street, but who was he to question the customs of the people? He just ate his fill and drank his liter bottle of beer until he dozed off on the back seat of his car. Minutes or maybe hours after -he couldn't know with certitude without checking his watch and his eyes were too dazzled to make this task an easy one to accomplish- he was woken up by the rays of the insidious sun. That sun was starting to arouse a deep-rooted feeling of hatred in him. He felt the heat of his temples and earlobes before feeling the wetness of his back and smelling the rancid odor reeking from his armpits and groin. As soon as he recovered his coordination, he tried to escape from that hell, but the extreme heat of the door handle prevented him from carrying out his plan. He cursed a couple of times to gain courage while he took off his wet T-shirt and wrapped it around his hand. He opened the "hot as hell" door and exited into cooler air. He looked for the first shade he could find: he hadn't thought of shade while he was filling his stomach with chorizos and beer in the middle of a cool night nor had he thought of it when he'd lain down to rest his badly slept weariness. He thought about the car melting under the impassivity of the despotic sun, but he didn't have the energy or the inclination to move it from its place; he'd wait until night and learn for the next time that the fact that

49

the sun is hidden doesn't mean that the "son of a bitch" won't come back to bother you again. "Calm down," he soothed himself. "Calm down or you'll defeat yourself." And he could think only of going back to the chilliness of his beloved Poland; he thanked his good fortune he could do that with a simple blink of an eye. And there he was, back in his room in Poznan, but it was still summer and he didn't have a fan. "It doesn't matter," he thought scornfully. "Summer is so pleasant in this country." And indeed it was. No one complained about the sweaty journeys to their jobs on buses without air conditioning or about the odors that were exuded by some people who still hadn't embraced the advantages of deodorant. The Poles bore those inconveniences stoically as badges of their temporary happiness. Everything was preferable to the freezing gusts of winter.

Happiness is action and pain, are you ready for it my heart
or do you prefer the numbness of solitude?
Happiness is taking the blows and not trying to divert them
or to claim they weren't meant for you.
Everything's meant for you my heart; nothing's gratuitous,
and there where you put your treasure
you will find it later.
Happiness is pain and enthusiasm my heart, are you ready
to give up your illusions to gain freedom?
Happiness is here and now my heart,
it's this tear you drop today,
this disappointment that opens the door
*to new possibilities.*

## Chapter 11

"I don't want to see you anymore", he said, and maybe he did mean it, but he knew that to stop seeing her was going to be a very difficult task. He could try to understand this feeling by comparing it to the decision to stop smoking, but he didn't feel that simple psychosomatic dependence could explain what was going on in his mind and his spirit. He thought that it'd be more accurate to consider it all from an existential point of view; he knew that the act of not seeing her would be a demanding act for him, as it would require more willpower than going on seeing her. It'd be far from inactivity or paralysis; it'd be a positive act full of her presence. He'd have to hold to the lack of her as the source of the love he'd been looking for in her before. The lack of her would be full of meaning to him; he wouldn't be aimless or idle anymore; he'd have the hardest of tasks to perform. The previous lack of meaning in their relationship would be transformed in an act full of sense, the act of forgetting her. He thought about it all and repeated for the umpteenth time that he wanted her out of his life. He focused on the things she refused him and emphasized his despair by reminding himself of her promise to never change her mind about him. He wanted to put an end to all that senselessness; maybe by running away and hiding from her eternally; maybe by hurting her so much she'd see it wasn't worthwhile seeking pleasure with him. Because it was at those times when he was so upset that he remembered her lighthearted attitude in public, her merriness, her enthusiastic conversation and her smile full of suns. He couldn't have pity on her at those moments because he felt pity for himself; no matter how bad she was feeling or how many problems she had, he felt he was the victim in their relationship. He couldn't take it that she wanted him to tell her that he was content to be just her friend. "What would either of us gain from that?!" he shouted back. Could he really stop desiring her by a simple verbal commitment? He couldn't, even if he put all his will into it. He felt that his desire needed to be torn away; it couldn't be just appeased by wishful words. However, the next day, while still at work, he was happy that she paid no heed to his tantrums. She was coming over to see him and everything would be as usual; that was all he wanted for the time being; that was all he longed for while he waited to go back home and make some preparations for their meeting. He'd stop at a supermarket and lingered in the aisles, waiting for his inspiration to kick in and tell him what to buy for the occasion. Maybe some orange juice; a bottle of wine would be capital, but wouldn't it create a drinking habit between them that he wanted to avoid? Occasional wine was great, but drinking wine habitually was more than pathetic. Yes, orange juice would be fine, but she didn't like bottled juices; she said they were full of preservatives. Maybe he'd buy some oranges, then, but they were so expensive. He wondered why bottled orange juice was cheap then; maybe they made that juice out of apples and just added the orange flavor and colorant. Who knew what the ultimate reaches of science were?

He bumped into his pretty colleague in the office kitchen; she exuded sensuality from her eyes and cherry-like mouth; she was always in a dress and her white legs and neck protruded from the dress's folds and her neckline. When they had just met, Miguel had tried to hit it off with her, and she'd shown interest. He'd chosen movies for a topic and she'd reacted really positively. She had made an effort to remember which movies she'd seen that weekend and her suddenly blanking in front of him had struck him as cute, but everything had crumbled when she mentioned she'd seen the movies with her boyfriend. He hadn't been so eager to talk to her after that and now he limited himself to polite greetings and some small talk if they happened to be in the same place for longer than a minute. But she was still interested in him and when she got hold of him, she didn't let go of him so easily. However, eventually she finished the conversation by saying "I'll go back to my work," as if trying to convince herself that she had something else to do other than chatting with him.

Back at home, he tried to kill time while he waited for Luiza. Many things had happened between them. Miguel was thinking about her sweet oceanic blue eyes and her diaphanous smile. They'd gotten very close the last time they'd seen each other, but now he was back to his regular life. He had a job to keep his days busy and a book by Victor Hugo to entertain his mind in his leisure time; however, he still found a lot of free time to think of her. He made up a song, recorded it and then sent it her in mp3 format; then he arranged some verses into a poem, which he dedicated to her. He could feel it was going downhill and he didn't know whether things could get back to the way they'd been; for all he knew, their most golden time had happened that last Friday they saw each other. She'd seemed so vulnerable, so needy, and he'd felt so strong and necessary; it was going to be difficult to get rid of such a strongly imprinted sensation. He didn't want his life to be *Fifty Shades of Grey*; he wanted to be led by more than basic instincts, but deep inside he knew he wasn't above it all. The desire for possession was still one of the main drives in his life. He was more than human and that was the toll he had to pay to be a writer. He saw everything through the magnifying glass of his mind and emotions. Things got out of proportion and a simple act of inconsequential flirtation could be devastating to him. A lighthearted girl who sought his company to spend her free time could become the reason for his existence from one day to another. His capacity to project was as powerful as it was harmful to him. He'd suffer for a girl he'd just met as if she'd been the companion of his life for years. His idea of love was so utterly hopeless; it was an idealist love and it didn't seek any compromises.

Luiza had cried in his arms; he probably meant more to her than any other man in her life, but that was nothing to him. Like an anguished freedom fighter that decides to put a bomb in a public building, Miguel couldn't help defeating himself. He couldn't see any other way than his way, and his way was hindered by reality. He'd lose and he knew it, and he knew the only thing to do was to stop troubling her with his manifestations of unrequited affection. What were all the pages he wrote about them to her? What did "them" mean to her? Was there even a possibility that the pronoun meant something special to her? He knew he wasn't himself without "them" anymore, but was it ever going to mean the same for her? He'd almost obliterated himself just to exist in the plural form, while she had a double existence, as "she" the individual and "she" the occasional "them".

Fortunately, the other aspects of his life had good prospects. He had a bearable job; he'd succumbed to the neo-slaverist system, also called neo-liberalism, which promulgated eight daily hours of paid resignation of your freedom, based on an exploitation system already denounced by Marx, which squeezed the life-energy out people who, in neo-liberalist terms, were mere assets in the economy of a country. A society so constructed that hours of freedom were another commodity to buy and not the natural state of humans, who had the sad privilege of being the only animals on earth that had made having a family a second priority, a pastime between working hours.

However, his "masters" were as lenient as white slave-owners can be. They demanded the production of intellectual commodities from him, so he was spared working as a field hand. He was a pampered slave, a slave with a monthly allowance to be spent on activities to pass the time between the periods of his confinement.

He was earning relatively well and he was putting money away to buy a flat. Like any descendant of immigrants, Miguel had a propensity towards acquiring property, in contrast to the European propensity towards adventure and discovery. Like most people from the Americas, Miguel's economic efforts went towards the acquisition of personal possessions and real estate. The European fondness for traveling was seen as little more than an adolescent whim by him or, as it was commonly seen in the

Americas, something exclusive to the upper classes. Because the instinct of possession is so rooted in the American mindset, an American who travels is sure to have a mansion to come back to from his journey so that he will not envy the wealth of the places he's been to. Americans are so bewildered at European hobos traveling around, maybe because they haven't read enough of Jules Verne's novels or maybe because they haven't incorporated the word "well-traveled" into their dictionaries. The most plausible theory is that Americans are Europeans who have already gained the achievement of having explored and conquered a new continent. What need is there for them to explore any longer when they're already living in the New World? They have nothing more to do than to lay back and see the fruits of their entrepreneurship ripening.

He knew he was in love and that there was a karmic imbalance between them, or at least a discrepancy in their interests. She was interested in getting to know him better and he was interested in gaining her affection; these aims didn't oppose each other, but they were in discord sometimes. As his ultimate aim was union, he saw the distance between them as a threat and an ominous signal, but, as her aim was to simply know him better, she saw that distance as a necessary means of objective observation. Whenever she deliberately distanced herself from him, he fell into a crisis and, whenever he pushed too much, she felt overwhelmed and coerced into a decision she wasn't ready to make.

He knew he needed to stop weaving plots and imaginary webs between them, but he knew that was impossible. Maybe he'd sublimate it all by writing about it, using his feelings as the source of his inspiration. But how to write properly when he was too immersed in his own fable to be able to be transcendent? Did he want to transcend after all? Or maybe he only wanted to understand his life and to learn to live it without hiatuses. So why to cram his mind with fictitious characters when the only thing he wanted was to get rid of emotions? How would a fictitious character channel his unfulfilled desires? Would he make his female characters as he wished Luiza to be? Would he develop a character with Luiza's features, but with a greater inclination towards him? He thought that would be breaching a writer's professional vow: never to try to change the world but to explain it.

And there they were again, at his place, conversing on whatever topic they found at hand. And there she was again, vulnerable on his sofa. And he cuddled her, but he was actually nestled up to her. She'd requested the warmth she needed and he'd given what was only necessary for him to give. She asked him not to demand more from her than friendship and the idea of demanding something else hadn't crossed his mind at that moment. There was a moment of conversion of interests while they lay on the sofa without uttering a word, without breaking the truce they'd both made with regards to their relative struggles.

There was one thing he was sure about; he was happy that this time he'd stayed around enough to allow the girl to show him her affection. In general, he rushed away as soon as he was rejected and tried to avoid the girl so as to make her regret her decision. But this one had clung to him body and soul. She'd given him no time to escape, as she'd monopolized all the exits. For a while he wondered what kind of sadist she was, but then he resigned himself to his lot. Now he was in a delicate position because he didn't want to do anything that could draw her away, but he wasn't as close as he wanted to be either. He found himself always in the margin between love and hate, but the fact that she showed herself consistent and that he seemed to be the only guy she was playing around with inclined him rather in her favor. He'd have to make do with what she was able to give him and wait patiently, trying to disentangle himself from inconsequential girls and situations, but while always keeping an eye open for the opportunity to fall hook, line and sinker for another girl like he'd fallen for her.

## Chapter 12

"Sovereign debt of sovereign nations cannot be collected by force"- Drago Doctrine.

The Glass-Steagall Act was born of an American law of 1933. The Act clearly distinguished between different types of banks by implementing regulations that prohibited investment banks from owning commercial banks or having close connections with them. The Act also restricted the scope of commercial banks by preventing them from dealing with securities. However, as early as the 60's, banks and other institutions made a determined attempt to blur the distinction between security products and banking by profiting from loopholes in the law and developing subtle kinds of financial products. This led to the repeal of the provisions in the Glass-Steagall act by the Gramm-Leach-Bliley Act in 1999.

Argentina had to face the consequences of its 2001 default on bonds issued under American law. One of the numerous American hedge funds, nicknamed "vulture funds" by the international community, took Argentina to court under American jurisdiction. They refused to accept the debt swaps offered by the Argentinian state and demanded full payment of the debt with accrued interest, even though they'd bought the bonds for a tenth of their value in a speculative maneuver. Argentina alleged that such a demand was a threat to their sovereignty and that, due to the fact that they had defaulted, they needed to restructure the debt and therefore they could not pay the full amount to the vulture funds without creating a liability which would lead to a new default. The main problem was a clause in the bond contract, called the RUFO Clause, that determined that all the bondholders had the same rights upon future offers. That meant that even though ninety-three percent of the bonds had already been brought out of default, if Argentina paid the full amount of the debt to the "holdouts," the rest of the bondholders had the right to demand the same treatment and this could create a snowball effect that would lead Argentina to a new default. This stalemate threatened to destabilize the whole debt restructuring process, as it was difficult for Argentina to close the deal without the agreement of all the bondholders. Many years before, Argentina had submitted to American jurisdiction when it chose to emit bonds under New York law to make them more credible. Now the American court ruled against Argentina and confiscated some money which had been transferred to an American bank with the purpose of making payments to the rest of the bondholders, who'd agreed to the debt restructuring. The decision of the court was based on an interpretation of the legal terms of the contract that supported the vulture funds. Argentina had chosen the clauses and the country of emission of its bonds and now it would be held responsible for it. When the country brought the case to the Court of Appeals of the State of New York, the court repeated the same ruling, saying that "a court is not free to alter the contract to reflect its personal notions of fairness and equity." The question is what 'personal' means for them. Aren't we dealing with persons when we need to cut pensions and the social welfare budget to put more money into the vultures' pockets? If being personal is a weakness, why do we have feelings at all? Why aren't we just soulless automata that can't distinguish between right and wrong by themselves but need to be programmed to do it? Is this where humanity is heading? Many countries and institutions around the world expressed their solidarity for Argentina. The more people know about the background of the debt, the more empathy they feel for this country. The bonds that were bought for a song by thes vulture funds have a dark origin. They were born of the country's most abominable dictatorship. The Argentinian junta borrowed massive amounts of money in the most careless way, while they kidnapped and made people disappear in the most careful way. In the five years of the dictatorship, the foreign debt rose tenfold and the country was driven to a dire economic situation. The country could've refused to honor the debt because its origin was illegitimate, but they were under pressure from the IMF and other creditors to honor the debt and so they did. The IMF was a very privileged scourge of the country; they advised Argentina to enter default and then gave them some austerity measures to be applied in order to squeeze the money out of the nation. The country paid off the debt to the IMF and thus got rid of its nefarious influence.

However, solidarity may not be enough to bring down an unjust system. The democratic system around the world is jeopardized by the laissez faire economic attitude of the countries that have the greatest say in it or, in other words, conscienceless people are allowed to do evil due to the indifference or lack of courage of the global society. These vultures have faces – they are companies led by single men. Single men can be brought down by the intervention of a country like the United States. Rules can also be made to stop other vulture funds from praying on countries and thriving on the misery of nations. The positive evil these kinds of companies exert menace the security of the entire transatlantic financial system. Argentina, as an economic ally of the United States, has been driven away by the negligence of the American government. South American nations are starting to form links with the Asian Pacific region, Russia, China, and others. It's high time the Wall Street tycoons were replaced with an international financial system and the United States were driven towards Glass-Steagall bank separation in order to destroy the speculative apparatus that has sought to effectively eliminate national sovereignty by means of money and law suits.

In Europe, the devastating effect of this global policy is also felt. Efforts have been made to bail out a select few financial institutions and large banks while at the same time the population of the planet is being destroyed with austerity measures. Responsible and honest economists believe that this system needs to be replaced with Federal credit for productive employment and a return to national banking, and that the payment of illegitimate debt needs to be abolished. "This gambling debt, which is like betting on a horse, should be turned into credit," Alexander Hamilton argued. Due to tricks and maneuvers, this derivatives bubble forced sovereign nations to pay again and again, and this "banker's arithmetic" eventually produced a debt bomb. "All the illegitimate debts need to be audited and written off", was the unanimous voice of human economists. Once the aggregates, which are mere derivatives, are wiped out, ninety percent of the debt is gone. These derivatives are mere bets to cover loses, with no legitimate financial obligation. The nineteenth century cannon must be discarded and new policies of productive physical economy must be favored in America and Europe, as they have been in Asian Pacific nations. The financial system needs to be geared to permitting the development of the productive powers of labor in the respective economies.

The imperial forces, however, would rather threaten to blow the world up than yield power. The Syrian, Iraqi and Ukrainian wars were an example of interventionism as part of a global struggle to force the Russians and Chinese to back down. The other warfare was subtler, but more efficient and consisted in forcing the whole transatlantic sector to sink into financial chaos. The Commonwealth is still exploiting other countries whenever possible and they don't want to yield control. The United States needs to resume control over their own country, implement a banking reform, wipe out Wall Street and catch up with the global market, now led by the Asian Pacific region. The Americans needs to dismantle the hyper-inflated economic system governing the occidental world. As DeRousse once said: "It's Wall Street or mankind."

The American court said that justice existed to apply the law, not to forgive trespassers, but what about crimes against humanity? Weren't the Nazis exerting a legitimate right by implementing a national policy against an evil detrimental to their sovereignty? Wasn't the Holocaust a civil and international war in terms of law? Wasn't the principle that all crimes should be subordinated to the pre-existence of the law undermined by the trials of the German National Socialist Party's members?

"Nullum crimen, nulla poena sine praevia lege poenali." By applying a punishment without a pre-existing penal law, were they creating a chaotic legal system or were they just following a natural instinct for justice? What is justice in this case, just a toy wielded by the current kid in power? If men could take justice in their hands when dealing with crimes against humanity, why couldn't they see that law is not a guarantee of justice at all but a mere fence to show burglars where their criminal prospects begin. The legality of an atrocious action is what makes it sinister; otherwise, the Holocaust or dictatorships would be regarded as mere savagery, just like Viking raids or indigenous human sacrifices. But the fact that these acts can find a loophole in the legal system and that, in contrast, a mere boy that robs a man with a kitchen knife is sentenced to three years in prison in Argentina is sad. The fact that a whole country is brought to its knees by one unscrupulous vulture fund boss and his suit of hyenas, the fact that this is evident to anyone except the person who makes the legal decision, this scission between reality and law, between justice and legality, between doing good and following orders, all this senseless Roman circus ends up with something more unfair than the mere law of the jungle – all because of what is enshrined in statutory books.

**Chapter 13**

Miguel's girlfriend had been offended. Luiza had stayed for a week at his place and during that time she'd become his girlfriend. He didn't need to ask her; although she hadn't deigned to tell him that she wanted to be with him, the state of affairs was evident. He was afraid of touching on the subject, in the same way as an admirer of Da Vinci is afraid of touching the Mona Lisa, lest he blurs an eye or erases the nose by mistake. But she was his girlfriend for the time being, at least in practice, which was the only thing that mattered. He had a great capacity to build on illusions; like creating a fictitious character in a book which then becomes the narration of your own life. She was flesh and bone but she'd always have something of fantasy in her, something with soft edges that dissolves itself when you're too eager to grasp it and which surrounds you but you can never possess.

The point is that she'd been offended. His landlord was too present those days and he wouldn't give up on his right to reign whenever he had a chance to. Although he was a personable man, his whole demeanor changed once he crossed the threshold of his property and he adopted an air of easiness which reminded Miguel of roosters strolling inside their pens. He had many things in his head; he was a busy man and his visiting the flat, though never welcomed by his subjects, was an act of magnanimity on his part. So there he was, wasting the time he could've spent making hundreds of zlotys, just to go and see how his subjects were doing. He'd rule and pass judgment on them, solving domestic disputes caused by someone forgetting to wash away the line of dirt that forms in the bathtub after a bath or by someone bringing their partner to stay over for more than two days. So it was only natural for him to expect his rulings to be obeyed in his entire realm and therefore to extend over every person that entered it. And there lay the problem; Miguel didn't think the same. He'd submitted to his rulings as you submit to a stampede of cows crossing in front of you. He just let it play itself out and then he resumed the coherent and sensible life he was used to living. But he wasn't ready for the grotesque scene he was about to see being played out

62

in front of him. Like a horror movie that has no meaning for someone who's not a fan of the genre and who interprets it rather as a dull comedy or a bland drama, the actions performed by the king became worthy of a fool or at least a royal peacock displaying its feathers.

So the thing was that Miguel's de facto girlfriend was in the bathroom when there was a visit. A girl had come to see a free room in the apartment and along with her came his majesty. They were waiting to see the bathroom as the last attraction in the tour of the house. His majesty was getting upset, maybe at his royal time being wasted or maybe simply out of boredom. As many nobles tend to do, he threw a tantrum just for the sake of entertainment. As soon as Luiza came out of the bathroom, all this pent up royalty saw a reason for its existence and felt an urge to be released. He stopped the poor girl, who was traversing the corridor swiftly to go and put on some clothes. He addressed her and demanded an explanation: what she was doing? Was she was staying at the place or not? Then he recited the rules of the kingdom to her, clarifying the point that a stay longer than a day should be notified. Luiza shut the door that led to Miguel's room, maybe so as to prevent him from getting upset hearing the mistreatment she was suffering or maybe just out of pride, to prevent him from seeing her humbled. Miguel was busy giving a video lesson at that moment and his first impulse was to drop what he was doing to come to her rescue, but then he thought that, as she'd shut the door, she'd decided to deal with it by herself, thereby showing her self-sufficiency and the resources she could bring to the relationship. In an act of deference to her emotional intelligence and social skills, he decided to let her deal with it by herself, reasoning that his intervention, rather than being helpful, could be detrimental to her aims at that moment. He'd actually heard her giving excuses to the landlord and he thought everything was being solved smoothly, but he didn't reckon on her pride. He didn't imagine the titanic efforts she was making to keep her composure in front of such a caricature of a man. He didn't count on a woman's ability to control her emotions and check her sensitivity in the presence of a brute. But when she came back to the room, her demeanor told him he'd misjudged the situation and the blood immediately rushed to his heart. That heart was soon pounding vehemently, its riotous beats echoing through his whole body. He tried to keep calm and asked her matter-of-factly what the brute had said to her. Nothing out of place had happened, but her emphasis on his rude manners and his raising of his voice compounded the fact that he'd burdened her gratuitously with his presence. The landlord had already gone away, but when Miguel saw him again a week later, he remembered the injury that had been done to his girlfriend and he simmered with indignation. The next day, he wrote him a message.

In Polish, there's a linguistic form of deference which is ubiquitous, even when asking for directions in the street. For a Polish person, it's something so incorporated in their culture that they simply accept this kind of treatment without the slightest change in their attitudes toward their interlocutor; however, for Miguel, because of his modern upbringing, this kind of treatment sounded too formal because it built a formal barrier between the two interlocutors. Therefore, he deliberately adopted this formal Polish form: "Pan", which literally means "lord", but which is translated into English simply as "you," because of the lack of a formal form in this language. The e-mail he wrote to his landlord was in Polish, but here it's translated into English with this small nuance. Therefore, the form "Pan" takes the shape of "the Lord" to better convey Miguel's intention, although it might have been overlooked by the addressee. Here's the transcription of the letter:

*I write to the Lord because I wish to deal with a delicate issue, which I need to explain well, and I would not like to cause the Lord to be upset. I would like to ask something personal from the Lord, and the Lord alone can decide whether I'm right or not, and decide what to do, too. I would not like to offend the Lord and I'm sorry if I say something that upsets the Lord. I know the Lord is not in the best mood sometimes, and there may be many reasons for this, for example, something broken in the apartment, and so on. I do not seek to be treated nicely by the Lord – that depends on the nature of each of us. I know that I'm not communicative or open and therefore it's hard to talk with me. I would like only to remind the Lord that every complaint the Lord has about me should be addressed to me directly. I'm referring to my girlfriend who told me that the Lord shouted at her. Although she is sensitive and I know the Lord has the right to behave as a landlord in his own apartment, it was not nice for me that one of my guests, in particular my girlfriend, had to endure being punished for something that was not her fault. I would like to ask that, if the Lord cannot behave hospitably in front of my guests, that the Lord at least do not talk to them. I need to remind the Lord that the Lord's wife came and talked with me and I behaved as nicely as possible, even though I was not in the best mood. I expect the same treatment from the Lord. I hope that I do not cause a lot of trouble and I am always ready to accept that I am wrong in my conjectures, but I will not tolerate such a situation being repeated, so I had to inform the Lord. I thank the Lord for his understanding.*

## Chapter 14

*Quelle minute funèbre que celle où la société s'éloigne et consomme l'irréparable abandon d'un être pensant! Jean Valjean fut condamné à cinq ans de galères- Les Miserables*

Miguel was anguishing over the situation in his country. He couldn't take it that the world should be only about money, even to the point of some numbers in an account being more important than the wellbeing of nations. This reminded him of his job and he started wondering whether the couple of cyphers he received monthly in his account were worth anything at all. He knew at least what they meant to him, full months of work and at least six hour a day of typing French words on his computer. Two hundred zloty represented a whole day of work to him, so everything was measured according to this amount. He always discounted automatically the fees of the virtual mortgage of the apartment he wanted to buy, which amounted to around forty percent of his earnings. So he was left with only sixty percent of his earnings. A dinner for two in a normal restaurant was at least fifty zloty, which represented twenty five percent of his daily earnings, and that was too much to pay for food. Eating at a fancy restaurant was simply out of the question. Movie tickets for two, around forty zloty, were a luxurious twenty percent of his day of work, and they generally didn't pay back their value in terms of wholesome entertainment. Traveling was the worst imaginable thing for him. You need to spend money on things you have at home and you're more careless with your money in a week than you are during a whole month back in your place.

He'd decided to be careless with his money at home from time to time, to fill the void of the sporadic need to be a profligate, but he'd always be careful with the way in which he squandered his money. He felt a duty towards creating a healthy economy. He'd buy fruits or vegetables whenever he saw a promotion in a supermarket or they were in season; he would by no means buy expensive food because he just didn't believe in it. Everyone knows that global hunger is a problem of organization and distribution. The tons of staple foods that are wasted in a consumerist society could feed many people who aren't as picky when it comes to their meals. Miguel did not believe in letting potatoes and onions be spoiled in a Polish supermarket while he bought himself some Italian salad. He used the same principle mothers use with their children: "Finish your potatoes first and then you can eat your Italian salad."

Something that astonished Miguel was the fact that bananas imported from Ecuador and bought at the supermarket were cheaper than strawberries cultivated in the village and sold on some street stall. He wondered how they offset the cost of transportation and distribution. If he was paying 4 zlotys for a kilo of bananas, how many groszys was every Ecuadorian plantation slave receiving? Was Poland deliberately contributing to making Ecuador a banana republic or was it only that Poles didn't know how to plant their own bananas? Maybe a new variety of cold-resistant banana was already on its way in some Polish lab, but for the time being Poland had to resign itself to being the last link in a slave-trade chain in order to have a taste of this tropical fruit.

But what bothered Miguel the most was the vicious cycle people created by traveling during their vacations. He couldn't avoid thinking of money as the driving force of the world whenever he thought of the budget for a journey in summer. The worst thing of all was that the European air companies were inflating people's illusion that traveling was a healthy economical activity by offering cheap flights everywhere, while exhausting the oil reserves of the whole world. Everyone knew that oilfields were going to be depleted by 2050 unless they started searching on the moon, but no one seemed to know how to stop squandering oil. That's how the vicious-cycle modern economy traps us: as we don't know how to fix the problem, we'd rather just take advantage of an economic boom when we can. He wanted to stop the economic karma at least during his vacations and start the countdown again after he'd rested for a good while. He was lucky because he spent all his time abroad, but he knew he needed to visit his parents or send his future children to Argentina from time to time. He saw no means of breaking with this karma because he didn't want to get completely detached from his origins; he wanted to keep a link with Argentina. A round ticket home for only one person was about the same as a whole month's work; it was simply an insane number.

He needed to stop thinking in terms of numbers or he'd drive himself crazy. He'd gained two kilos since the last time he weighed himself; he should focus on that. This was a wonder because since time immemorial he'd had the same weight. Even after his stomach operation, when it had taken him two weeks to go back to his normal eating routine, he'd lost only two kilos which he'd gained back in a few months. Now he'd just suddenly gained two kilos in a couple of weeks. He'd checked his weight two weeks before and it was his usual one. Maybe the vitamins he was taking had helped, but he thought it was more probable that the new diet imposed by default when she came to his place had contributed more to the increase in his body mass. He'd always wanted to gain weight naturally; he'd been underweight his whole life and a couple of kilos more would suit him well. Now he probably would look healthier and his relatives would tell him he looked fatter, which was considered a compliment to men in Argentina. But yes, he was fatter, which was a sign that he was enjoying himself and was happy. The body doesn't lie and he had to accept that that girl had improved his appetite; he couldn't deny that fact.

However, the demands, always the demands! She was all he wanted in his life, but he felt he outreached himself. He couldn't cope with her and that frustrated him; he couldn't satisfy her completely. It felt like covering holes with his hand. They were fine up to a certain point, but sometimes he felt that tension that's a hint that if you take a false step, everything will crumble. He felt he couldn't control himself at certain moments and that he'd destroy everything he'd built with her. He had a tremendous power, the power of self-destruction, in his hands, and sometimes it was too much for him. He felt endowed with the usufruct of her body and he exerted his right to take its measurements, exploit it and eventually rip it apart and reconstruct it in a cycle of fits of passion and care. However, most of the time he wanted to be by himself, without worries or responsibilities, thinking only abstractly without a reality waiting for him.

And there was also another life for him, the subconscious one. He never could remember his dreams so he missed out on the full-fledged parallel world his mind created while he slept. In this world, he traveled constantly to Argentina and sometimes he couldn't even come back to Poland; those were actually nightmares. His subconscious mind was aware of everything that happened in his life and included the updates in his dreams, but his subconscious also believed strongly in the reality of its own created facts and it didn't want to give up on them. So in his dreams, Miguel's real life was mixed with these imaginary facts, which took more relevance sometimes. The fact that he had applied for studies at a Polish university was combined with the illusory fact that he often visited his parents, so now he was in Argentina and needed to come back to his studies in Poland, now he was rejected by the university and had to go back to Argentina and now he was crying at home because he could not go back to Poland. The strange thing is that, in his dreams, Miguel remembered he'd just dreamed all his journeys to Argentina, but the verisimilitude of everything that happened around him was so great that he couldn't help believing that this time, as well as others, he'd actually been in Argentina and that his other life, his sedentary life in Poland, was the actual illusion. Thus, his mind gave him a fierce battle. His subconscious was like a man that once, when he was a child, saw a horse painted in blue and now believes that all horses are blue; he sees other horses, brown, bay, white and even black, but never again blue; however, he reasons that all the horses he sees are just exceptions and that his rule still applies: all horses are blue.

*You're taxing my strength,*
*everything grows weary beside me,*
*you tax my impulses, my living force*
*to accommodate them to your fancy.*

*My freedom to desire is taxed*
*by your ideals of love and life*
*and I'm depleted of all I have*
*and the only thing I have left*
*is to make of it a gift to you*
*which is unworthy to your eyes.*

**Paraphrase of Sen by Janusz Rozewicz**
*First they were red, and then became blue*
*speckled small flowers, fragrant ridicule*
*then they flew around, passing off as butterflies*
*and the butterflies cried that they were full of lies*
*"they have the gall, such an impudence, we can't stand this falsity"*
*while they sank with the flowers in golden luminosity*
*I saved them from the abyss, it would've been so tragic*
*They were blue, and red again and beautifully magic*

*I hear you snore from the depths of your dreams,*
*when you're on the verge of falling into a luminous abyss,*
*and you'll get up and breathe and saunter around*
*with the majesty of your sovereign steps,*
*and I wonder where your steps will lead you this time,*
*to which continents and spheres, terrestrial or celestial,*
*for when I write about you, a part of you gets detached*
*and falls into my pages, away from me and from you*
*to become as remote as the thought of you*
*snoring placidly in your morning dreams.*

## Chapter 15

They were walking along one of the most commercial streets near Stary

Rynek. All along the street and on both sides of it there were cafes that tried to stand out from the crowd, not through glamour or splendidness but through originality and character. The façades of these cafes were no more than ten meters long and they were quite simple, but once you entered one of these places, you started feeling their coziness. You felt invited, almost obliged, by their warm atmosphere to spend a reasonable amount of money. They couldn't make up their minds which café to go to, which one would be less expensive, when she mentioned that she'd been on a date in one of the cafes. Chance had brought them in front of the place that reminded Luiza of a guy she hadn't found interesting enough to concede another date to. "He asked out me for about five months before I granted him a date," she said proudly. Miguel didn't know if the guy wasn't handsome enough and, if he wasn't, he didn't know why she'd even granted him a date in the first place. She'd mentioned he wasn't interesting, but what did this word mean in female terms? He remembered many dates and many girls who he'd had a very good time with and who never had time for a second date. He also knew that even a girl who agreed to see him a second time might not be interested in a relationship; for all he knew she might just be killing her free time or trying to "make a new friend", which is the code word for: emasculate a man. However, he couldn't explain why these girls who seemed to have a very good time with him refused to carry on seeing him. There it was again, that incomprehensible breach separating him from womankind. Had Luiza also acted as if she was happy in front of this guy she rejected later? In any case, Miguel was happy she didn't mean the world to him and that he could afford to not be interesting to her; he'd just find another girl he could please in that case. At least he hadn't begged for five months to see her, he thought. And the idea came to his mind that he'd hate her if he'd wasted so much time on her just to be rejected. "And she was glad, for goodness' sake! She was glad of having wasted hours chatting with a guy

71

she wasn't interested in." Miguel really liked her and admired her, but he also occasionally despised womankind through her.

Every day we play hide and seek, and we still haven't found ourselves,
we play at politics and economics, and at being masters of our lives,
and rules are necessary to keep the game going.
But today we play at writing our poems on a blank page,
as we played at making breakfast this same morning,
and we play at loving and hating, till our games become professions,
and our poems are not a game anymore, and we love and hate in earnest.

## Chapter 16

Miguel was having some issues at his place. His flat mates had complained about him to the owner and he'd notified him that he needed to leave the place in a month. It was offensive to Miguel, but he didn't want to take the offense. Maybe they were right in asking him to leave; maybe it was the best for them all. He couldn't stand the bossy attitude of his flat mates either; they always had something to complain about. He wasn't the perfect flat mate, but he believed a flat was to be used and lived in, and that an occasional mess was inevitable. He used the place and kept it clean as if it were his own, but he didn't like cleaning it for others' sakes. So whenever the place was intolerable for others, he thought it was up to them to clean it up or to agree with him on the best way to deal with the situation, but not to boss him around. Maybe he was too disorganized to live with them, but he was fed up with their habit of unpleasantly telling him off whenever they didn't like something. He couldn't believe they took more care of having an impeccable house than of having a convivial atmosphere at home.

The day he received the notification from his landlord, he wrote the following open letter. It was open because he didn't give it to his flat mates. "They wouldn't care about it," he thought. However, he wanted to express his feelings and maybe he'd give it to the owner once he'd moved out and he'd ask him to give it to the girls in his flat "if he would be so kind". In that way he could make him read the letter too, because, although the owner knew it wasn't his fault that Miguel was being thrown out of his place, he still had the right to decide, as the owner, whether Miguel stayed or not, and he'd decided to do the easiest thing: throw out one of the tenants to keep the rest satisfied.

*If you like someone, you tolerate them.*

*If you do not wish bad to someone, you do not throw them out of the place they chose to be their home.*

*We live in a world of transactions, where cordiality lasts as long as a deal takes to be sealed.*

*We forget that we came into life to learn to live alone and with others.*

*I think that people are not merchandise that you can change if you do not like them.*

*I believe that every man, every sensitive soul, is worth the effort.*

*I think that I grow when I do not give up the opportunity to be nice to someone.*

*A small act may mean nothing for some: only a change of roommate and the hope for better in the future.*

*But for others it means lack of tolerance in a world that begins at home.*

*If we are not able to tolerate an occasional dirty sink, bathtub and other petty things, how can we find out what is really important: that each of us has a sensitive soul striving to be accepted.*

*For my part, I have nothing to complain about. I saw only nice people when I came here. It's a shame that others do not feel the same about me.*

## Chapter 17: On the death penalty and other petty things

Miguel had seen a documentary about a serial killer on the internet. He was called the Green River Killer and had murdered more than forty women throughout his life. Even when he was happily married he continued killing from time to time; it had become a habit for him. People obviously wanted to subject him to capital punishment – this was in the States – but he'd pleaded for his life in exchange of information about all his murders and he was granted it. During the whole trial, he was so cooperative and well-mannered that the lawyers and even the judge were astounded when they first realized he was the murderer. It was all thanks to DNA evidence; up to then the killer had succeeded in putting up an innocent façade. Once the proof against him was too solid, he walked into the courtroom and confessed. Now he was a sociopath, a killer as cold-blooded as the American soldiers in Iraq or the national soldiers who crowded the South American cities during the atrocious dictatorships of the seventies. He'd killed by sword and he deserved to perish by sword; he was blatantly demanding it, hiding this impulse from everyone, even his happy wife, because he couldn't stop himself from committing these crimes. Now there was a criminal you couldn't feel pity for, and they weren't feeling any pity for him; however, his life was spared.

There was another case, a kid who'd shot down three other kids and injured two others in a cafeteria. He wasn't a sociopath; he'd killed in a fit of rage, helped by the American law that promotes the ownership of guns as an inalienable right. Of course, adolescents get angry around the world, but not all of them have guns at their disposal. He'd obviously done it deliberately, as if fed up with life and totally disappointed in humanity. His was an act of revelry, a scream of freedom, but it's really sad this scream took up such a sinister tone. Like serial killings, this cafeteria shooting was part of the idiosyncrasy which is often found in Americans. This kid's scream of freedom could've been expressed in many other ways. In other circumstances and in a different environment, where he would've had access to other ways of expressing his anger and frustration, this crime

74

wouldn't have happened.

Hedonism is an unforgivable sin to criminals. The crime is more crudely perpetrated when the criminal hates the victim. It could even be said that all crimes are socio-pathological acts, all criminals are sociopaths. But society feels no pathos for them. All of them are ill people who need to be cured, but society decides to lock them up, to extirpate them as in a bad case of appendicitis. However, Miguel understood. Maybe because his mood had been set to understand loneliness when he was asked to leave his flat, maybe because there were many times when he felt he had nothing to lose, like most of those people. Fortunately Miguel still had his family, who supported him unconditionally, and a girl who'd chosen him to share moments of her life with. He wasn't lonely, but he knew the feeling; he'd failed to feel connected with life before and he knew how bitter it feels, how desolate. He had a huge imagination so for him it was a matter of projecting any criminal thoughts he'd had into multiple consequences. Perhaps without this capacity, he could've been an outlaw or a death row criminal in an instant. One thing he was sure of: he was as afraid of jail as a cat is afraid of water. It was a natural fear to him; he'd rather be a fugitive than spend a long time in prison. He'd do whatever it takes to escape such an inhuman situation. He couldn't stand the idea of being put in a cage like an animal; it was so degrading, so debasing. He knew that if he committed a serious crime he'd never surrender to the police but he'd die running away from them. His instinct for freedom was greater than anything else and he couldn't imagine spiritual freedom without its physical equivalent. He knew that, if he had to choose, he'd choose to break away from society rather than give up his freedom. But society is organized in such a way that leaves no room for breaking away from it. Materialistic people are so afraid of losing what they have that they make up rules just to prevent other people from wronging them. They don't' understand the universal laws of justice; they don't know that life is a risk we run every day and that rules are just a barrier against communion with the world. They believe that rules are just for animalistic natures who respond only to reward and punishment; they are behaviorists at heart. They want stability in their lives, so they ask: what would happen if all the animals from the zoo were freed? What would happen if we had no rules to contain our basic instincts? But actually legality is a prerogative of those who can always find other means to fulfill their desires.

Miguel had displayed contempt towards the law many times; he'd transgressed all the laws he thought to be unfair. It wasn't until he'd embraced a law that he followed it; he never followed a law just because it was legal, but because it was moral. For sure no one wants to get fined for walking across a street with a red light, so at those moments he avoided being seen by the police, but he didn't believe he was doing any good to society by standing there like a fool while no car was passing by. He thought that when he got old, he'd wait for the green light because he didn't want to run the risk of being run over by a speeding car, but while he still had nimble limbs, he could afford the risk of dodging a car driver lured by a green light as if it were a red rag and he were a bull blinded by rage.

## Chapter 18: Matters of money

Miguel remembered a few money issues back at home. He recalled, for instance, the time when he'd found a hundred pesos as he was walking out of his school, which was called the School of Fine Arts. He was with his mother and sister, and their mindset was temporarily influenced by the fact that his birthday was a few days ahead and they were planning a small party. To say a hundred pesos nowadays is not to say much, but back then they were equivalent to a hundred dollars. So, to say that an eight-year-old kid found one hundred dollars in the street is not to say little in a country like Argentina. His mother had to use all her power of persuasion to gently take the money away from this kid who'd never had such a sum in his hands and who wasn't even aware of all the possibilities it implied. As the kid had no real notion of the value of a crumpled piece of printed paper, he didn't give much resistance to her entreaties; he agreed, reluctantly at first, negligently in the end. He soon forgot this event, which was inconsequential for him, as he wasn't aware of the importance of an action that had given a week's economic relief to his mother.

On another occasion, another matter concerning money was being discussed, this time with his father. His father wasn't thrifty like his mother; he was rather careless with his money. He'd promised to pay for a trip Miguel had to make with his Karate school. The trip was to the capital, to compete against kids from other provinces. Miguel had been preparing himself for this competition for several months and he'd been training intensively for the last few days. His father, however, always used to run out of money by the end of the month and luck had it that the trip took place a few days before he received his monthly salary. He was also very persuasive, as persuasive as the mainstay of the family can be. He talked about bills to pay, some of which were due months before, and he didn't need to stretch the truth because he was right, Miguel's family was always a little in dire straits at the end of the month. The expression: to make ends meet wasn't a metaphor in their case; his father took care to make it a literal expression. So by the end of the month his father didn't have the money he'd promised Miguel when he was relatively wealthy, that is to say, at the beginning of the month. Maybe out of habit, Miguel's father hadn't put that money away but just expected to squeeze it out of his pocket when necessary. Now was the time to squeeze it, but he wasn't really eager to do it. It was a considerable amount, one hundred pesos again. His father had the money because he never broke a promise. But it was his intention to talk Miguel out of going on that trip. Miguel felt the weight of the guilt of depriving his family of peace of mind and economic stability, but he withstood it and pondered the dilemma with the help of his inner moral balance. According to him, the fault was his father's because he'd already promised him the trip and it was his reckless management of money that had created the difficult situation they were in. Miguel didn't tolerate the wishful thinking of his father in the slightest and didn't forgive him for the negligence of promising something he couldn't fulfill. As a merciless creditor, he saw the matter in legal terms and his father aroused no sympathies in him. He listened to his father's arguments with attention, and, in the end, like an impassible judge who's used to his task, he found against his father and gently took the money from his hands.

## Chapter 19: The tram shooting

Miguel got on the tram and sat on one of the back seats. The tram was somewhat full, but not like in the rush hour. Ten seats ahead of him there was a husky with its owner. It was muzzled and it kept leaning against its owner, rubbing its back against her leg. Whenever the tram started up or slowed to a stop, the dog got startled and crouched against the woman's leg, getting most of its body under the seat. Miguel couldn't see the dog; he was busy reading a book and taking glances at pretty-faced girls, as usual. However, he could hear a slight murmur that grew into exclamations and shrieks of despair in a matter of seconds. He couldn't see the cause of the rumpus, but he could see where all the glances were directed to, so he instinctively turned his eyes into that direction. The tram was in full movement, but people had gotten up from their seats and were dispersing from the focus of attention. When the place was cleared, Miguel could see what it was all about: the dog had set itself loose; its owner was shouting at it while she tried to grab it by the hind legs. The dog had managed to tear apart its leather muzzle in a fit of madness. It had also managed to slash open the legs of some trousers around it and to snap pieces of garments away from their owners. The only thing it hadn't managed to do was to bite a four-year-old boy standing entranced two meters away from it. His wide-open eyes couldn't stop staring at that phenomenal beast with fangs the size of his fingers. His mother had abandoned him in an act of absentmindedness which she wouldn't forgive herself for for the rest of her life, and he was deaf to the shouts of people who ordered him to get away from the dog. No one had dared to approach the boy and rescue him from the claws of the demonic pet; all of them shared the same feeling, the thrilling expectation of a catastrophe about to happen. They had already calculated the years of prison to be given to the dog's owner: "manslaughter" they all thought, "and she won't see daylight for a few years; and well she deserves it for not restraining such a cold-blooded murderer; maybe she gives it too much raw meat, etc, etc." The mind is incredible swift at a time like that, and some people had already envisaged the whole picture, with scenes of the American judicial system taken from some TV serial, for want of real material to fill their imaginations with. But the dog didn't deign to bite the kid, and people started to get uneasy; the dog was the scapegoat for their lack of courage and their petty excuses for abandoning a kid while escaping from danger. Some of them thought of their own kids and reasoned that it'd be negligent to put themselves at risk and eventually deprive their children of a future without one parent. Others told themselves apologetically: "Where's his mother anyway?" and they put the blame on her for being such a coward and extended their contempt to the kid, who deserved to pay for the consequences of his mother's vileness, according to their subconscious beliefs.

The dog wouldn't even bark at the kid; he didn't represent a threat to it but his eyes actually reminded it of his little master. It saw no more reason to panic, as the tram slowed down to a regular stop. The driver hadn't even noticed the incident; he was thinking of the beetroot borscht he'd had for lunch; he thought he'd never tried such a delicious soup, and this for only five zlotys. People got off the tram to resume the monotony of their lives; however, they all had an interesting anecdote they couldn't wait to share with someone. Maybe they would play mysterious and nonchalantly announce to their boyfriends or girlfriends that they had nearly died in a murderous incident. Of course, they'd exaggerate their own courage and develop the evil of the beast to its full potential. In some stories the beast would kill some and injure many; in others, it would be condemned to be put to sleep. None of the stories would linger too much on the fact that they'd done nothing to prevent the kid from being slit open by sharp fangs. Some of them would immediately kill the boy for the sake of saving themselves the trouble of answering questions such as: "Why didn't anyone do anything to save the boy?" or "Didn't you see the boy before?" They'd answer without missing a beat: "He was dead by the time I saw him." or "Many people tried to unclasp him from the jaws of the beast, but their efforts were fruitless." And everyone would be left with the feeling that there were no actual weapons against the evil in this world and that they were defenseless against terrorism of this sort. They'd also try to blame it all on the promiscuous violence on TV, which apparently had some influence on pets too. They were happy to declare that mad dogs were a reflection of a decadent society and nodded their heads in grim approval.

## Chapter 20

*You will know them by their fruits.*

"Hi Steve," said Miguel. "What's new in your life?"

"Nothing much, I've been to my parents and then I've busied myself with the Church, and you?" answered Steve in a monotone.

"I have a job now; it's the first time I've worked in my life! Well, I've done freelance work before and this job is not full-time. It's kind of freelance too, though I have to show my face at the office from time to time."

"Nice to hear you're making improvements in your life. Come what may, you're gaining experience in the only career you can ever succeed in: life."

"And how can I win in life's career, may you be so kind to tell me?"

"Yes, I may. You need to set a pace first; you don't want to get too tired before it ends."

"But doesn't it end when I reach a certain goal? That's the whole purpose of a career, isn't it?"

"Yes, but you aren't allowed to see the goal in this career, so you'd better set your pace as if to run a long marathon. This career is not measured in length but in time."

"You know what, Steve? I'm a little sick of the obscurantism of our age; sorry to change the subject. It's not you but what you represent that upsets me. You know that people have always philosophized as you do right now, but that hasn't improved society. It's positive things that improve society, like electricity for goodness' sake! The internet, like it or not, has given opportunities to millions of people, without mentioning the fact that it has made information available to everyone. How come you can be so retrograde at such a moment? It seems that you're only objective is to counteract the effects of positive science by dimming things with your rhetoric."

"It's not rhetoric; it's the simplest way I can find to express what I think. What do you mean by obscurantism? We try to bring light to the world. How can you say something like that?"

"We're in a new Dark Age. I believe that future generations will look back upon us with contempt and their textbooks will classify our times as the Modern Dark Ages. The high levels of fanaticism show a retrogradation of society, which veers away from knowledge and science and snuggles under the covers of religion. What's this new habit of professing to everyone that Jesus is your Lord or that Jesus is great and stuff like that? You want to combat superficiality by mouthing meaningless things like that?"

"It's not meaningless to me; it's actually the only meaning of my life. Why can't I profess it? Must your evolved world become intolerant towards something that doesn't hurt anyone and can save many?"

"I'm just saying it's not aesthetic. Of course I won't hate you for saying meaningless things, but if you want me to take you seriously, you must accept my criticism. Otherwise I can remain quiet, but don't ask me to consider you intellectually equal to me."

"Ha ha! You're funny, man! I went through college. I didn't shut myself up in a monastery and make up voices who told me what to believe in. I've had similar life experiences to yours; only I decided to take the Lord's path. Won't you allow me to do that without considering me your inferior intellectually?"

"I allow you to; just try to be clearer when you profess your beliefs. Try to make it more exoteric, so the lay people can also understand, ok?"

"Ha ha! For sure; I'll work on that. Nice to see you, Miguel. You're always a good surprise to me."

"Nice to see you too. You're disturbingly stimulating; intellectually speaking, of course. But let me know when you have some free time and we can meet up."

"No problem. Now I must go. See you next time."


## Chapter 21

Miguel was having trouble fitting into the Polish working pattern. They are born to harsh weather and need to thrive under difficult conditions. Being indoors is already a dear privilege in a country where being outdoors means catching a cold or getting the flu or pneumonia. His boss wasn't satisfied with his work and he resorted to the old formula of an authoritative tone and threats, as endorsed by every Polish householder since the beginning of time. Miguel came from a climate that encourages rebellion, be it only because it is so hot and damp inside that people feel uneasy staying in. So Miguel wasn't used to having his usual restlessness, the product of excessive temperatures, exacerbated by patriarchal remarks and threats of being thrown out of the house. He'd gladly go outside at the slightest excuse he had to take offense, be it an annoying fly that had taken possession of the room, a parent that had just started shouting or the lack of regard and respect for his individual freedom implied by the fact that his parents had ordered him to do some chore. He wasn't Polish so he didn't enjoy the privilege of a cozy house where he could shelter himself snugly from the uninviting cold outside. Fresh air and a light blue sky were a continuous invitation to break free from all the bonds society likes to burden us with. Breezes of freedom were breathed in by every Latin-American person from their early youth and therefore they found it difficult to put up with the restrictive rules of northern Europe.

He was badly paid, like the majority of Polish people, but it was actually a deservedly low salary. They'd hired him months before to do some search engine optimization work, but they hadn't actually let him know. They had hired him under the pretense of needing a copywriter and he'd accepted gladly. They'd actually given him a chance and for a few months he had dedicated himself to writing – he was actually paid per word. But in the end reality showed its fangs and Miguel started being paid per hour, as a regular employee, and he was given extra tasks which consisted of promoting the website. He couldn't commit himself fully to his job because the website was just another product to sell, another website that tried to attract as many visitors as possible just to earn some money which would be spent on other unnecessary things, the ever-spinning wheel of causality. However, if he stopped thinking of numbers as mere economic profit, he could enjoy his job. Whenever he thought that a great amount of visitors was a sign of recognition for his work and that they actually profited from reading him, he felt immediately rewarded whenever he saw the number of visitors increase.

## Chapter 22

Leo was waiting for Miguel with a couple of beers. Miguel didn't like beer, it actually felt heavy on his stomach, but he accepted the drink Leo offered him as a gesture of friendship. He wasn't drinking much from it, though, so Leo started pouring it into his own glass. Miguel found this gesture even friendlier than the previous one, because it meant there was trust between them, that a glass of beer was communal between them and that his friend was humble enough to steal from the beer he'd just given him as a gift.

Meanwhile the conversation had taken a dark tone. Miguel was full of doubts about Luiza; she wasn't so attractive anymore; she'd lost her original charm for him. It was so confusing to realize that something he'd fought for with conviction had now become a valueless trophy on his shelf; he'd dreamt and been kept awake, struggled and cried for something that now had lost its appeal to him. Maybe he was nothing more than a warrior and his destiny was to fight to the death, to die by the sword in the thrill of battle. He didn't want peace; he enjoyed the alertness coming from his unfulfilled desire, from his hunger. He didn't want to be full ad nauseam; he preferred lacking what he wanted the most: a woman to share his life with. And after all, he had no idea of what it meant to share his life with a woman. He'd thought of the nice things a woman represents; he'd thought of the delirium of fresh-scented soft skin wrapping around him the whole day, with sweet eyes to look at and playful hips to chase around the street and the house. But he hadn't thought of the effort this would imply because he hadn't looked at it as an obligation but as an optional passion. But now that he was in a relationship, he couldn't opt out of things he'd seen as pleasant once, but which suddenly became compulsory. To chase her hips wasn't a pastime anymore but daily work, lest she should be dissatisfied. Her sweet eyes always showed him something else than what he wanted to see; they were sometimes also tinged with bitterness. He'd claimed her love as a gratuitous thing, but when the time came to give back some of that free love, he'd had second thoughts about it all. Because he wasn't ready for generosity; he was going through a period of selfishness, a period of eternal adolescence in which he wanted to become fruitful in his writing. He didn't want to do what was right but to write about it. He wanted to advocate for happiness and wellbeing from a position of sadness and wretchedness.

"I'm a teacher who doesn't apply his own teachings," said Miguel.

"But at least you're a master," jeered Leo.

"I mean, as Luiza said, I'm not looking for a woman but for an object to masturbate with."

"Wow, man! She said that?"

"Not in those words, but I got the hint. That's why I don't feel attracted to her, because I don't feel the need for bonding. I live in isolation and I seek pleasure and happiness in solitary activities, like reading and writing, do you understand? I'm a closed system; I don't allow the world to get in."

"Well, man, you're an artist. Artists are always aloof. I think it's imperative for you to suffer to get inspiration for your work. I think you seek personal depletion rather than fulfillment."

"I don't know what to do with her; I want to make her happy, but she isn't happy with my halfhearted dedication to her. She feels I'm not giving her my whole being and it's true. I'm reserving my energies for my work and I'm cheap with her, only giving her enough to subsist on. I'm not able to give myself completely to her or to anyone. I've never done it and I don't feel I ever will."

"Yes, I know. You're unbalanced; you seek so much intellectually and you despise the flesh, as all religions do. You're intrinsically religious, you knew that? Even though you don't belong to any dogma."

"Maybe. Maybe I have a philosophical yearning towards dissatisfaction. You know my most creative moments are the ones in which I'm going through a process, and now that I've found what I wanted, I'm stuck. It's like madly trying to catch a firefly and now that I've done it, I just yearn to let it free again and see its beauty away from my hands. What in heaven's name do I want with a firefly anyway?!"

"Fireflies are useful creatures, Miguel, you just can't see their full potential. They can illumine your life. It's true; you've been so focused on other things that you don't see the obvious. Don't worry about anything. Everything comes in its due time."

"I don't know; I feel I prefer darkness because I have too many defects to go out into the light."

"Maybe you're too proud to seek out help and you prefer to suffer in silence than to cry out your weakness."

"Maybe, Leo. Maybe I just don't know how to phrase my suffering. Maybe I haven't learned to cry yet."

"I hope you'll learn soon."


### *Paraphrase of Neruda*

*I can sing the saddest song tonight,*
*I can sing, for instance, a Chico Buarque song while I dance a samba in*
*honor of your watery eyes, and your tears drop to the wet grass.*
*For once, out of the love for all things, I made a paper flower for you and*
*you treasured it as you treasure your nails, your hair or your shoes.*
*But as a useless sun that shines when it's uncalled for, I shined away my*
*desire, just to rise again, but in other fields, warming the fruit trees that will*
*give fruits to be gathered, giving sunstroke to some young lady or making*

raisins out of succulent grapes.

Other suns will loom on your horizon and many stars will remind you of a remote paper flower, and the grass will still be wet, but your cheeks will be dry already.


### Paraphrase of Andrés Calamaro

I saw you burning your eyelashes before a dream,

sitting on a wooden bench, amid trams and quiet passersby.

It looked like heaven had open the door to us together,

I'm always your friend, though I wish you well,

just don't expect consistency out of my inspiration.

I can't be proud of much, when everything I did was to find you,

I can't be ashamed of little, when I left you as you were that day.

I gave you many things off the record,

now I need them back with me.

It was as much of an honor to meet you

as it's now a shame to part with you.


### About conquerors and conquered

Today I met your eyes,

as usual but deeper in color,

and I palpitated in excitement,

as usual but louder,

and put a thorn into my heart

to remind me I'm not immune

to pangs of euphoria and ridicule.

About conquerors and conquered,

today I met you once again,

as usual but darker

full of the hues of my dreams of happiness,

*and I was subdued once again,*

*as usual but faster,*

*for when defeat is inevitable*

*the only victory is to surrender*

*and tell the world I've been conquered*

*as usual, but willingly.*

## Chapter 23: Science Fictional

Miguel was at a farmers' market. Green onions, cucumbers, pumpkins, many kinds of cabbage, green onions, parsley, onions, fruits and apples, red apples everywhere. Miguel saw more things than he knew the names of; it looked like an alien island to him and he didn't feel like exploring that day. The only thing he could gather from this all was that he didn't have enough money in his pockets to prepare himself a proper meal with these vegetables and fruits; they were so expensive. Except for the national staple: potatoes,  apples, cabbages, onions, carrots and seasonal fruits and vegetables, the rest were exorbitantly expensive. He was thinking of the vitamin pills he'd got at a pharmacy for 50 cents each. Those magic pills had every single nutrient that gold seekers try to dig out of farmers' markets, and even more. He was consuming more vitamins and minerals than he knew the use of. All the range of vitamin B, plus some other letter; he wondered why they hadn't arranged them in alphabetic order at least, so he could know which one he was missing. He'd started taking vitamins since his mother had told him that the lack of them might be the reason for his sleepiness. Miguel had been reluctant at first and had read dietary articles and researched the properties of all the food he'd ever eaten. He saw that he must spend the day eating to fulfill the standard dietary requirements. He saw for the first time the seriousness of the grand dilemma of panda bears, who generally choose eating rather than copulating. Unfortunately, his instinct of procreation was stronger than his need of self-preservation, so he'd chosen the shortcut of ingesting a supplement every day. He also bought yellow cheese and meat, for he couldn't dispense with that; cheese because it had calcium, for which the daily requirements are so high that it's inconvenient to fulfill them with a daily tablet, and meat because it was easy to cook and had enough iron and protein, meaning that he would not have to worry about fainting in the middle of the street. He still avoided consuming flour or simple carbohydrates, like rice, corn and kasha. He replaced them with potatoes, which were cheaper and had some minerals, though in very small quantities. Maybe that was the future of society: flavored vitamin enhanced mashed potatoes for everyone. At least people wouldn't be worried about caries or other teeth problems anymore. He also bought chicken, because it was the cheapest meat available and it had more protein than beef or pork. However, he got easily fed up with chicken and he needed to go back to pork, for beef was too expensive. The days went by in this fashion and, with an apple a day to keep the doctor away, Miguel just needed a blender so as to make nice milkshakes out of those cheap fruits. That would solve his daily disorientation as to what to prepare for breakfast, for who in his right mind could reject a nice jug of milkshake for breakfast?

It was not his fault that chocolate bars were cheaper than oranges; he liked them both, but he also knew their relative prices and he wouldn't buy oranges if he saw they were expensive. He'd given up on his second favorite fruit, except when it was in season; his favorite fruit, grapes, had always been seasonal and expensive, so he bought them anyway whenever they were affordable. Eating had become an art of combining available food with the talent to prepare it into an edible and nutritious dish. He was slim, though, so he tried to eat as heartily as possible, but he was also a bohemian, which meant that he'd fast the whole morning if he wasn't hungry enough to make himself breakfast.

He'd read about synthetic food in some science fiction books, but he'd actually seen it in many products he'd consumed since childhood. Back in his country, he'd always drunk bottled and powdered milk indifferently. He actually preferred powdered milk because he could add more spoonfuls to make it tastier. He'd recently learned that they add back the vitamins milk has after they dry it up. Up to now, he didn't know that this was synthetic milk, a product that had lost all its proprieties just for them to be recovered artificially. It was just like making orange juice from orange essence with added vitamin C; he actually also drank those kinds of products. Where did science fiction start for him? He didn't know anymore. He just knew that people who need to send messages to the stratosphere to have them bounce back to a friend's cellphone so as to arrange a meeting or just say hi are on the verge of, if not beyond, science fiction.

When you go to bed today and look at your day's labor
and your thoughts aren't fixed on the gains of tomorrow,
when you smile at, shout at and insult the same person at the same time,
when your heart's not divided between foes and allies,
and you don't need any parties, for the world is a feast,
nor societies, networks, all your petty fears,
and you dance with the beauty and meet with kindred souls
and you cry and suffer to your heart's content,
when you stop counting on people's applause
and you're ready to be your own defeater,
when you win true victories which humble you to mud
and admit that two sweet eyes are worth all your values,
when you rage for no reason and rebel in comfort
when to be or not to be won't be a question.

## Chapter 24: On how the third world war was avoided.

He hadn't read a book in months; the training routine was overwhelmingly time-consuming. They were made to wake up at six, train their body resistance, their discipline, their resilience to harsh conditions, their discipline, their tolerance of fatigue, their discipline, their survival instincts... He didn't have a minute's respite from training and war indoctrination; however, he felt prepared to go to war at any moment. Anything would be better than that state of being without being which was promoted at military schools. So much torture can be seen only at universities that overwhelm you with theorems and hypothetical problems you'll never face in your professional life. It was tiresome, especially the monotony of the routine, which had become ingrained in his everyday life. Their only free day, Sunday, was dedicated to a sort of idleness you can find only during war times, when soldiers have a break from the bloody battle. And, however, there was something in his soul that hadn't been changed, his self-awareness. Yes, he existed and his internal flame was ever radiant, even incandescent due to the harsh experiences he was going through. It seemed that his consciousness of himself grew exponentially in relation to the physical and intellectual deprivations he was suffering. His soul had grown bigger than his intellect and it seemed ready to blurt out of his body.

Then came days of recurrent monotony and again those stupid attack and defense drills. They seemed to be training robots, but these robots had souls that flamed the brightest due to their lack of liberty. When the troop was polished and no flaw seemed to be found in their maneuvers, when at last they performed as if guided by remote control, they were given their final orders. They were supposed to be transported by drones and parachute land in a surprise attack on Russia. The government had decided to grab the bull by the horns and launch a preventive attack. But Robin was aware of the implications of this attack; he'd been trained for it. There'd be an immediate reaction by Russian soldiers and they'd try to repel the American forces, which by then would've already taken over the country. There'd be rebellious insurrections which must be quenched and that'd be their main task. The advantage of insurrections was that they caused the major harm to the rebels, because they were already under the invader's radar. Robin knew all this by heart because they'd been revising anti-guerilla tactics for the last three months. Robin knew these insurrections would involve civilians rather than professional soldiers, which meant easy victories for the well-trained American troops. The casualties on the invader's side would be minimal; as usual, America knew what war was all about and had taken the easiest way.

Robin wasn't even afraid of dying in Russia; he was as sure to live as he was sure Americans would go on eating hamburgers the next day. However, there was something that convoluted Robin's guts; his mind was blank and he could not think of any logical reason or of any metaphysical theory, but he was sure what he was going to do was wrong. This feeling was as tremendous as the void which guided his everyday actions; he was as sure as a tree is sure to stretch out its branches; he was simply sure that his call wasn't to go and invade that country and kill those people; he was sure his patriotic duty was done and he should go back home.

When his superiors heard his crazy idea of leaving the army, they threatened him with a dishonorable discharge and the loss of all the privileges and rewards he was promised as a soldier. He paid no heed to this and other compelling words, like the ones addressed to his sense of patriotism and belonging to the greatest country under the sky, to his love of democracy and freedom and his commitment to the American liberationist cause. He was immovable in his decision so he was sent back home without even his wages, but not without three months of imprisonment for disobeying direct orders. However, this penalty couldn't be applied because at the same time, in the heads of thousands of

American soldiers, the same idea had formed and they were resigning on mass from their military duties. Some of them were following others' examples; some were convinced by their own intuition that it was the best thing to do. Thousands of soldiers were dishonorably dismissed from their duties in the following days, and the newspapers that had already printed and even published the news of an imminent Third World War to be triggered by the American global security plan had to delete their news from their websites or release immediate copies of printed material taking back all they'd said supporting the campaign. A war that failed in its making was worse than a lost war, because it didn't even have enough honor to be considered a just cause. So they gradually or abruptly took back all they'd said and became the first promulgators of a nonviolent approach to the "Eastern Issue".

**Chapter 25: On the Falkland issue**

Miguel had just published an article on the internet. The internet has the particularity of promoting polemic issues, so this article was noticed by various people, some in favor and some against his ideas. This was an open letter to England, a letter he was eager to deliver:

*I want to start by saying that I'm Argentinian. Now, having said that, if you're English, you can choose not to read what follows, because my current feelings don't allow me to tone down the message, but if you're kind enough to read without taking offense, here's how an Argentinian feels about the Falklands.*

*We're portrayed by you as a deluded, stubborn nation, which we actually are. The propaganda shown in your media is so accurate I can't believe you don't see it; you talk about it, make fun of it and still don't get it. You make fun of our calling you "imperialists", when actually there lies the key to understanding the whole issue; the rest of the matter is pointless. We don't discuss who the Falkland Islanders will be better with, or even whose country is more developed; with that argument England and the US should just take over the whole world and prevent badly organized nations from governing themselves. We don't discuss either who discovered and successfully settled the islands; for your country has put much more effort into building the US, Australia, and other Commonwealth nations, just to see them become independent countries later on. The problem here, and this is the only thing you must understand, is that we don't want your country's imperialist face near our borders. I pity all your country's colonies and neighbors, especially Ireland, and I don't wish the same luck to ourselves. We couldn't be further from each other as nations; unfortunately, you belong to a country renowned by its piracy skills and we're recognized as one of the world's barns. We don't want a proxy country near our territory. The Falkland Islanders are under your country's wing and as long as English politicians keep their overbearing tone, we aren't interested in easing their way to neo-colonialism. I think the problem is that your leaders are so used to being called imperialists that now they just take pride in it. Your country has exploited and devastated a whole world; it's done a thousand times more harm than Nazi Germany, and it isn't as stigmatized as that regime. I think if your leaders had the decency of at least being humble when it comes to your past and if they at least tried to compensate for the years of exploitation suffered by my country, we could be friends as nations. As you see, it's not about economics or even political issues here; it's about love and hate, and we Argentinians hate the guts of people who colonize first and then try to seek democratic ways to stay in power. Having said that, I want to make clear I have English friends; it's just your foreign policy and whole patriotic fable I'm against.*

## Chapter 26

Miguel had been dancing and drinking too much lately. It seemed that

Bacchus was exerting some influence on him. He had his mind fixed on finding himself a good girl. Everything seemed fair enough to him, for he knew that nothing's free in life and that he needed to seek in order to find. However, he suffered a setback when a nice girl, one who could actually fit the description, told him that he seemed desperate. That statement came as a reaction to his confession that he went to dance in order to meet girls. He didn't see anything strange in this comment, for balls are social events and not a mere opportunity for the deployment of rhythmic skills on the dance floor. Besides, he thought he was immune to criticism as he was a good dancer and it was evident that he had put some effort into honing his skills.

He accepted the fact that he was desperate, but he couldn't see the point in her telling him. He felt it was more courageous to recognize his weakness than to mask his real intentions from himself and others. He also thought it extremely superficial to dance just for the sake of it, so he actually felt a rebellious stirring of his spirit at hearing her criticize him for doing something with a purpose rather than just having superficial fun. For a moment he thought of sending to hell every single girl that likes dancing, but then he resigned himself to the fact that women will always pay attention to forms and manners, although they appreciate sincerity. So he'd been direct and she'd chastised him for it, but he didn't care much about it after the offense had passed. He just hoped she'd give him some respite from her questions about dancing techniques; he didn't know why she wanted to make a point of it all; as if he were to think less of her for meeting him after he'd uttered that sentence.

Fortunately he knew he wasn't desperate; at least not in the sense she implied. He was thirsty for knowledge and for beauty, but he wasn't as superficial as that girl had made him out to be. She'd interpreted him from her own perspective, in which dancing was an enjoyable pastime. She couldn't understand that he spoke from his heart when he had tacitly confessed to her that he cared nothing for dancing, but that he wanted to go on seeing her, but he wanted to bypass all this folly – dances, dates, appearances – and take her to the core of life, to conversations about God and the future, about dreams and crude reality.

At that moment he remembered that Luiza had talked about hell during their conversation; he'd let it pass, although he'd thought of interrupting her to give her his opinion on hell. She'd swiftly changed the subject and he hadn't had the chance. That evening he told to himself the phrase he'd have told her:

*There are good non-Catholics and there are bad Catholics and anyone can go to hell. Of course God exists everywhere, even in the church, but we can always find him at home too. There is no heaven or any other place than life. People learn to live and life doesn't end with death, but it repeats itself ad infinitum. There are no evil people, only people who haven't learned to live yet. We don't go to hell as a punishment; hell is a state which everyone can be in, even if objectively they may seem to have everything they need to be satisfied. Hell concerns us all and is within us all. There are no sins, just mistakes. There's no guilt, but our actions have consequences so we need to think next time we're doing the same thing. Guilt does not exist as a feeling; that's why it's taught to children; it's a value, but it's not natural. The only natural approach is simply to understand that everything we do has some effect and to learn to accept the consequences.*

## Chapter 27: On Polish culture

What's so elusive about the term culture? Culture is easily defined by its etymology; it's all the material and non-material things we cultivate during our lives. People from different nations like different food, so they grow different crops and therefore have different cultures. Every individual also has their own culture, as everyone has in themselves the power to choose which of their experiences will germinate and blossom and which ones will be smothered by weeds. So if every single person has their own culture, which differs from all others, can it be possible to define the idiosyncratic culture of a nation? All attempts to do that would be full of generalizations, conceptions which may be well-founded or not; for instance, that climate shapes people's characters. However, the observations of an unbiased person, although tinged by his conceptions of psychology, may be useful if we compare them to the observations of other unbiased people in order to describe the general character of a nation.

By unbiased we mean someone who hasn't had any conception of the particular nation prior to his observations. It's important then to define the culture of the observer, as it's the tool by which the second culture will be measured. In this case the observing culture is Argentinian, and the culture observed is Polish. To have a more objective analysis, we need to describe in the observing culture those features that we see in the culture being observed. In order to do that, we'll resort to a third culture which will represent the common opinion on Argentinians. This culture doesn't need to be analyzed, but it will instead be considered as the "world culture", although such a thing doesn't actually exist.

The world culture says that Argentinians have big personalities, that they're generous and friendly and very talkative. They would talk to you for hours on end and it seems they have all the time in the world to make your acquaintance, invite you to their homes and feed you. They're loud and effusive when they speak, even when they talk about trivial things like football or music; many of them have a personality and will tease you and mock you in a friendly way.

They can seem impolite in their manners, especially towards strangers, who they treat very casually, even patronizingly. They can be deceitful, consciously or unconsciously; they'll make a commitment and then decide whether or not to fulfill it. Out of their conformist nature, they'll always act enthusiastically about anything you propose to them, so you can never know when they're in earnest. They're a very proud people, but this is an individualistic pride, emerging from every one of them, and not from their sense of belonging to their nation; actually, they are not patriotic at all, except when it comes to football and women.

There are many artists among them and most of them have a bohemian trait. Argentinians don't like working much and go on strike as often as possible. Many of them look for alternative ways of living and venture into street art and craftsmanship or they just live off the state. All of them once wanted to be famous football players, musicians or NASA engineers, but they seldom have the willpower or the inclination to realize their dreams. In the end, they content themselves with a small house, provided it's full of kids and friends.

They live with their parents till they marry, and sometimes even after they're married, if they can't afford their own house. They seldom leave the comfort of their parents' nests before they graduate and have a job. Argentinians dress up whenever they go out, but always keep a casual look; only at very formal parties do they put on a suit or high heels. They often go out; they start out very late, as discos open around 2 am in Argentina. It's very normal for them to party until dawn and then sleep the whole day. They dance gracefully and mainly dance in couples; they also have no problem in making out in front of everyone. Couples kiss on the dance floor, in parks, on the bus and everywhere you can imagine. They eat lots of beef and pasta; the typical Sunday dish is roast beef and, if you're lucky, some leafs of lettuce and slices of tomato. People are slim till a certain age, but no one's shocked to see their partner put on considerable weight once they're married; actually the most commonly used word of endearment is "gordo" or "gorda", which means fat.

They're so friendly that their word for friend has lost its intensity there. But they're always creative enough to come up with new words of endearment. They'll call you "primo"- cousin, "vieja"- old woman, which stands for mother, or even "marido"- husband. When addressing women, they most commonly use names, although in general they tend to use nicknames derived from anywhere: a cartoon, a thing, or some onomatopoeia that's associated with that person and which has stuck because of its originality. It's not uncommon to have two or three nicknames, one in the family and others among friends.

The Argentinian culture says that Polish people are shy and formal, but kindhearted and very honest. They practice brutal honesty, so if you do something they don't like, you'll receive their immediate disapproval, without any sugarcoating. They're socially clumsy, with unpolished manners, but they're so candid that it's impossible to dislike them. They're reserved when they speak in public, but they can be loud after a couple of beers or in the intimacy of their homes. They're very nice to talk to because they're respectful towards their interlocutor.

They are a hardworking people. They study and work and don't complain about scandalously low salaries. They can rant for a long time about the weather and how beautiful life would be in France or Germany, but they will rarely go on strike or just quit their jobs whenever they're dissatisfied. Some of them can be depressing with that passively gloomy attitude they have towards life.

They are very independent. Children leave home and support themselves as soon as they can. They're paradoxical; they like going to study as far from home as possible, but always within the boundaries of Europe, because they say they'd miss too much if they lived too far from their parents'. Sometimes they go abroad for a whole year or more, but they always come back to their family and friends, as their sense of belonging is generally in Poland.

In the street they walk very fast, as if fleeing from a snow storm. They look straight ahead of them, and their voices take a vexed tone whenever

99

they have to stop and tell you "przepraszam" when you're in their way. This word, which means sorry, is abused everywhere, on trams, in shopping centers, etc. They will say it loud and clear to you, which will add offense to injury, as if you were a kid that's horsing around and aren't as busy as them.

They're very patriotic, but they love foreigners and foreign languages. It seems that since the globalization party started, Poles are loyal attendees. You can trust their honesty in virtually everything. They're very strict when it comes to respect towards others. You'll be surprised at the commotion you'll create by simply taking some food from your flat mate without telling them. They'll also give you back every penny they've borrowed from you, but they aren't much used to sharing a drink or food. Almost everyone drinks from their own bottle and cooks their own food in Poland.

Polish people dress up for work or for going out, although they often pull on a pair of jeans for everyday occasions. There's a conservative tendency in female clothing; girls wear high heels on a daily basis. They can start drinking very early; it's not uncommon for them to have a beer at 5 pm and by midnight they can be already drunk; they also have no problem going to sleep like angels after having drunk a shot of vodka.

There's an astounding variety of sausages there, the famous kielbasa. However, they're fans of Arabic Kebabs, which they've customized to their taste with a lot of cabbage and other vegetables. They also have many varieties of soups and salads, which may be the reason why they're so slim.

They have degrees of friendship. If you meet someone for the first time, don't expect them to call you their friend; you'd rather hear the word "kolega", which in Polish culture has evolved to mean someone who's between an acquaintance and friend. If you've got yourself a Polish "friend", you can be sure it's a lifelong deal. Their nicknames are already conventionalized; you may even find them in a list. At the beginning, it's difficult to get used to the huge amount of Asia, Kasia, Basia, and their declensions.

## Chapter 28

*"Nothing is not the opposite of everything, it's its complement."*

Miguel met Leo at a bar in the Old Market. He wasn't in the mood for drinking, so he didn't do it; he just sat there and twice turned down an offer from Leo to buy him a drink. Beer also had an unsettling effect on his stomach and he didn't like the aftermath of alcohol in general. It had a marked stimulant effect on him, but he didn't want to abuse of it because he knew that, in the end, this effect was offset by a general despondency. So if he was going to be despondent – and it was the right time for despondency – he could just go home and find something more interesting to do than numbing his sensitiveness.

"How're you, dear?" was Leo's common greeting, even to male friends. Like every Italian, he was a little touchy-feely and, as he couldn't exploit this trait of his when addressing Polish people, he took out his pent-up excess of affection on Miguel. Miguel didn't mind; it was nice for a change to taste some of the warm treatment he'd gotten used to himself back in Argentina.

"I'm fine, and you? Long time no see"

"Yes, how are things going with Luiza? She looked distressed last time I saw her."

"We're not together anymore. I decided she wasn't my type."

"But she's cute. All cute girls should be your type."

"I know, but we're missing something. I'm missing something"

"Well, in that case, just look somewhere else and you'll find it. Coming to the party tonight?"

"Emanuel's party? I don't feel like going. Those parties are too full-on for me. He's always coming up with something new and alluring, like this Caribbean beach party in the middle of January, but his ideas show disregard for real communication among people. He doesn't cater for people like me, who prefer quietness and peace of mind to noise and excitement when meeting people."

"Ok, but you must admit his parties attract quite pretty girls. You said you wanted a good- looking girl for yourself, so what better way to find one than by sparing a little time to chat with one or two girls at the party; you may find someone that interests you."

"I don't know; I don't want to build on sand. I know there may be a chance that another lost soul like me goes to that party in the hope of finding someone, but that's not who I am, and I wouldn't like to meet the right person while I'm being something I'm not."

"But we, party people, are deeper than you think, Miguel. We have layers; there are some superficial ones which fulfill a superficial function, but there are others that allow for friendship and even love."

"I'd like to strip myself of all this superficiality and lay bare my heart so everyone could see it. I don't need the rest; I'm happy just being totally honest with myself for one day. Happiness is such a tricky thing, you know? We look for packages: a good job, a nice-looking and smart girl, and then we buy it, with an extra trade-off once in a while. But that's the problem with packages – they may be handsome, but they're nonetheless just empty packages; what you see is what you get."

"So you won't buy anything then? What will you put all your money on?"

"I'll stake it all on writing. If I really believe in what I do, I won't need anything else. If I really believe I'm doing a service to people and not only blabbering my petty affairs. Then the reward will come and I'll just have to stretch out my hand to grab the low-hanging fruit."

"I like your strategy; it's a brave one and bravery is often rewarded," said Leo before the conversation was interrupted by someone who knew

Miguel from somewhere, who had just approached the table. Miguel couldn't remember anything about him except that he was the brother of a sexy acquaintance of his. They had exchanged some words when the humorous girl had brought her brother to a party she was supposed to go to with Miguel, and therefore willy-nilly Miguel had made his acquaintance. This time Miguel deliberately avoided smiling to discourage the guy from further conversation. The mysterious guy wasn't persevering that much, so he kindly bid goodbye to both of them.

Miguel and Leo went on talking about trivial matters, which made up the mass of their relationship. Miguel enjoyed Leo's talkativeness and Leo found a good listener in Miguel. Their conversation lasted in general for as long as Leo had something to say, plus a few comments and updates on his personal life on Miguel's part. But although Miguel said little, he had the logistic capacity to start from the essential but end up with idle talk. So Miguel was always able to give vent to his feelings from the first second he was given the word.

## Chapter 29: Thoughts of a single man

When I see terror in the streets of our city or in a far Eastern country, I sometimes think that those people are simply insane and that criminal acts should be prevented. I think I'd do everything in my hands to rid the world of violence and hate. But then I go to my job and work overwhelms me with petty concerns; I spend my time and effort selling a product or producing unnecessary things. I seldom build or create new things because it's been proven that nothing's new in the world, that everything repeats itself in a rut. So I focus on promoting old things like love and courage and I try to come up with new ways of saying and doing what has been said thousands of times before. But time for creativeness is scarce nowadays; time to enjoy myself, to come up with a witty phrase that can draw a smile on the face of that person I love. And I leave life aside to go to work and do what I have to do so I can come back home and enjoy the freedom that's left me with my loved ones. I care so much about them; I don't know what I'd do without them. I do know, however, what I do for them. I know that there are tedious hours at work and many unpleasant tasks, which I'd never planned on doing, but which are unfortunately part of the job. And I'm doing some things which are not illegal, but which aren't positive either. I know I'm not hurting anyone; my job brings me money and it doesn't actually do any harm. There are worse things in the world, like terrorism or natural catastrophes and I'm working for my family's sake. Then I go back home and sometimes I hear more news of horror in the world, in our country, our city; we just hope nothing of it will ever affect our families. I go back to work, back to the routine and these inane tasks I do are still there. But it pays the rent and I need to earn a living for me and my family. However, one day, when I come back home and I find them safe, as usual, enjoying their meal in the peacefulness of our home, I just happen to turn the news on and see the picture of a girl that's been killed in a terrorist attack. They never show a picture of the victims, why have they done it this time? Not enough viewers maybe; they'd do anything to touch our feelings…

And unfortunately they've done it; that girl reminds me of my little daughter. And what have I done to prevent her death? I've done nothing. I've worked myself out of my wits and she's still there, in the list of the disappeared. I've done nothing wrong, but I feel so impotent. How could I have prevented it? I'm just a man doing routine work at a company. Could it have changed something if I did a job more useful to society? Probably no, but I still feel guilty, because if I'm not helping anyone, who's helping those people who will end up being terrorists? Who's preventing hate and violence from seeping into a kid's world so he can grow into a rightful person? I'm hoping with all my heart that my kids will be safe, but am I making the world a safer place? These questions are useless; how could I quit my job? Should I put my moral ideals before my family? I just go to work and try to make up for the wrongs I've done; I just hope the good I do outweighs my lack of social commitment. The problem is that lately, when I go back home, I don't enjoy my family's company so much. I've been feeling like being alone lately; I don't know why. My wife says that I'm a little different than when we met; she says I'm a little insensitive now... insensitive, what a recurrent word! But she's right; I haven't noticed it, but she's right. Because at the beginning it was hard for me to get used to my job. I remember I was bored to death when I first started. But it's become so natural over time that now I feel I couldn't belong anywhere else. I just accept my job as part of who I am. Because I'm my feelings, my values and ideals, but above all, I'm the things I do every day. So suddenly I've become meaningless; all of a sudden I'm not that idealistic guy who once shouted, "Love defeats everything!" Suddenly I don't believe in myself anymore because I don't believe I can make any difference. Suddenly I'm already dead, like that little girl in the picture, because I can't find a reason why I should go on with this life, perpetuating it. In this world, where something evil can happen to innocent people while others are indifferent, I'm not willing to live any longer.

## Chapter 30: Chinatown

A new page in Miguel's science fiction book had just been turned and it lay blank for him to fill with meaning. Miguel was in the mood for scribbling down some impressions he'd had since he'd seen his first Chinese person back in Argentina. He'd just finished drinking his morning *yerba mate* infusion, which was one of the few luxuries he could allow himself. This was not so much due to the high cost of desalinized water but rather the pangs of conscience he had whenever he consumed a non-essential product. *Yerba mate,* as well as coffee and all kinds of infusions, had been labeled non-essential products at the last UN summit. The rules from this summit had a worldwide effect, due to the fact that the United States had deigned to join the Union, probably out of fear of being left outside of the global economy, since China and Japan had already joined. All this ascension fuss had started because the last block of the Ward Hunt Ice Shelf had melted; by then most of the coastal countries in the world had already been flooded and the rest of the world had rushed into an alliance with the least evil of the empires: the European Empire. Of course no one called it the "Empire", except for some anachronistic Star Wars fans; most of the voluntary members called it the United Nations, which was actually a very accurate term for this confederation.

Miguel was sipping his yerba mate in a last effort to recall some of the old times in his life. He still remembered when his father would drive for hours on end on a road that seemed to lead nowhere, surrounded by palm-trees and grassland. Now the landscapes had become bluer, to the dismay of farmers and ranchers. Nowadays the cheapest livestock was fish. Desalinization was an easy process and many people had their own desalinators, but Miguel had just moved into his new house and he hadn't bought one yet. He was aware of the urgent need for one, because he needed to provide his family with 5 liters of drinking water per day. He had no choice but to buy a five-liter jerry can of drinking water every day: a Chinese label; they didn't bother to translate it anymore. The company that produced his jerry can of water was actually French, but, as most of its customers were Chinese, it had simply adjusted to the language of the Union.

Miguel went out at last, time to go to work. He grabbed his bike and braced himself for a cold ride; it was the middle of winter. He saw the bright side of everything; the global temperature had risen and Poland wasn't what it used to be; however, it was still cold some odd days of the year. The trams worked well, but they were expensive, for there was no alternative means of transport and the law of demand had insisted that they become a luxury only well-off people could afford. Using cars or motorbikes had been out of the question since the last crude oil reservoir had been depleted. Countries had started investing in alternative energy sources since the beginning of the decline of petroleum, and they were doing well, but this had not proved to be the main issue the earth would face. Continuous natural disasters battered cities; hurricanes and floods started appearing where there had been none before. The water level rose and rivers were flooded with salty water. Food wasn't taken for granted anymore. Fruits, vegetables and crops were the first things to suffer, then livestock. Everyone learned how much water it costs to breed a medium-size calf; drinkable water was just too expensive to waste on animals. Everyone had been forced to become vegetarian, but vegans and vegetarians were as disheartened as before, knowing that people didn't eat cows just because they didn't exist anymore. On the other hand, people started broadening their tastes, as they wanted to grab the last piece of meat available on the market. Wild birds were shot down; every herbivorous wild animal was hunted and then even the carnivores. It was a feast for the palate, but it didn't last long. Now the science fiction stories that had been read years before didn't seem so absurd; synthetic meat started to appear. Meat essence production became a major business; plastic recycling also became very profitable.

Miguel had managed to cram Chinese in five years. It was a requirement for almost every job nowadays. No one had seen it coming, but Chinese people populated the whole world, or at least what hadn't been submerged. Everyone agreed on the fact that the Chinese were survivors; they had acclimatized to all kinds of weather and conditions and they did the hard work that needed to be done in the catastrophe-stricken countries. Contrary to other nations, like Europeans, Americans, Middle Eastern Arabs, Africans and the Japanese, they weren't belligerent, and unlike South Americans, they weren't lazy or inclined to idleness. They were a hardworking people that had earned their place in the new world. However, some people, probably out of envy or frustration at their own helplessness, just couldn't help comparing the Chinese to cockroaches, which were believed to be able to survive everything, even radiation. But the Chinese hadn't offhandedly become the most proliferous nation in the world; it had been the result of a deliberate and systematic plan: a postmodern colonization plan.

Miguel came back home after a long day of work. He could smell the aroma of a recently baked cheese and corn tart, which his wife had made. In the world he was living in, that was just science fictional. He didn't ask her where she had gotten the ingredients from or how much they had cost; he just ate with pleasure and wished with all his strength that he'd never wake from this fantasy. He started wondering whether he took enough care of her, whether she was satisfied with him. He thought he'd do something similar for her the following day; he'd buy her a flower. He didn't want to think how much that would cost him or what would be the use of it; probably buying her a new computer would be cheaper and more practical, but what did she want another computer for? Hadn't we had enough of technology yet? The same technology that had depleted our earth and had forced us to eat synthetic food. He was determined to buy her that flower, and he was determined to tell her he loved her, not because of the tart she'd made, for his heart wasn't even remotely connected to his stomach, but because she'd given a new sense to his life; she'd just shown him that he was still the owner of his own destiny.

At last Miguel closed his laptop and went to bed. A new page of his science fiction book had been turned.

## Chapter 31

"Luiza's in hospital. She's well now; she was lucky her flat mate found her in time."

"But what happened, Miguel? I mean, how did she end up like that?"

"She was upset, it's my fault, and she took too many pills; her heart stopped beating; the doctor said she was dead for a few minutes. We're really lucky; I'm really lucky."

"But why was she so upset? What made her do that?"

"I was ridiculously negligent in my behavior. I didn't think what I was doing. You know, when you're in a delicate situation, you always think that everything will solve itself magically, and then, when things start to go wrong you're already entangled in a such a mess that you can't make head or tail of what's going on. I was just shutting my eyes, waiting till the worst passed, and it ended up worse than I thought. For goodness' sake Leo, I feel evil."

"It's not your fault. How could anyone predict that kind of reaction? It was a thoughtless move on your part, but she overreacted. There are other ways to solve these kinds of situations; she could've slapped you and gone away; she could've grabbed the girl by her hair in front of everyone. Why did she choose the loneliest and saddest of reactions?"

"Don't talk like that. She's too sensitive; you don't know her. She's incapable of doing harm to anyone other than herself, and that's her problem. She doesn't know evil; she doesn't know how to deal with it. She's not prepared for someone like me. I should've stopped meeting with her a long time ago; I'm just of too weak character to make such a definitive decision. I didn't allow for her jealousy; I knew she wouldn't be happy to see me with someone else, but how could I have expected such a result? I'm a mess Leo; I'm a messed-up mess."

"Take it one step at a time, Miguel; don't let yourself be overwhelmed by the circumstances. It's just the messed-up luck you have; everyone would be upset in your situation, but you're by no means guilty of what has happened. You know, most cases of suicide or murder occur in dysfunctional families. The closer we are to people, the blinder we are. That was your mistake; you gave her no time to react. You raised her hopes and all of a sudden, she found herself in hell. You should've let her prepare her for such a situation; although we're never prepared for a disappointment; we always hold on to the last hope we have until it vanishes completely; it's our nature."

"Thanks for your support. It makes me feel good to pour this out, even if it's just for the sake of it. I'll leave her alone; I think that's what she wants. She didn't answer my calls and she didn't allow me into her room at the hospital. I just talked to her mother and tried to explained everything; I felt so guilty I couldn't look her in the eye. And poor Luiza; she wasn't made for this world. I feel an invisible thread links us."

"She'll be fine, I'm sure. And you too, try to think about something else. You can't do anything about it now. Remember she's not only a victim; she's dealt you some malicious blows too. You're both out of place and out of balance; you need to get that balance back."

"I'll try, and I'll try to help her as well or at least leave her alone so she can get a hold of herself. Ok, Leo, I must go to sleep now; too much alcohol in my veins and too many thoughts in my mind had wreaked havoc with my nerves."

"Have a good rest and you'll see how things start to look up. Bye."

## Chapter 32

Miguel started walking towards the Old Market. It reminded him of the way in which he'd met her, their long strolls near the cathedral and the discrepancies in their ways of looking at the world. However, everything had been so harmonious; she'd listened attentively to him and he'd been spurred by her odd views on love, sex and society. He'd found it very rewarding to annoy her with his teasing and he'd been made even gladder by the closeness he got at every instant. Who would've thought back then that one day he'd want to get away from her as suddenly as he'd gotten close? Now it hurt his morals, his emotions and even his faith to want to restrain the flow of feelings he'd let loose. He wasn't in a condition to negotiate a relationship with her; it had all gone out of control. He sadly saw the product of a great emotional effort collapse completely; he couldn't save anything, not a single room, not a piece of furniture of what had once been his most precious home.

He walked across Most Teatralny and walked across the park with the sleeping fountain; the vacancy of its benches and pathways in winter increased the unrest in his spirit. That was the path he'd chosen to walk through, literally and metaphorically; a path of barrenness and solitude. What would've happened? Was this the question he didn't dare to ask himself? However, that was the question that gnawed at him, persistently, relentlessly. The cold freshened his face and the wind beat at his temples in a vain attempt to recall him from his thoughts. Everything around him was reduced to useless objects that could also just be reduced to binary code; the only distinguishable shapes were the image of himself in front of her or beside her, walking or arguing, her tears, her blind jealousy and his fits of passion. Everything was behind him now, but it appeared neatly in front of him, as if the past wanted to project itself into the indefinite future.

His disturbed meditations brought him to a conclusion. He wouldn't kiss anyone he wasn't in love with anymore. He'd seen the grotesque image of himself becoming something he didn't want to be, being carried away by ephemeral feelings. He'd failed to be himself and he couldn't forgive himself yet; he'd need weeks of honesty to make up for his self-betrayal, his self-defeating attitude. He wanted to make peace with her so as to be at peace with himself. He needed to find a way to be with her without getting close. He wanted to be present in her life, but he didn't want his presence to have any extra connotation for her. How could he neutralize her romantic feelings for him? How could he, a man, try to tamper with a woman's heart?

What had he said to upset her so much? Surely it wasn't his fault; her mind had been stirred by her emotions and the light in her spirit was dimmed at the moment she did what she did. Sometimes when they met, she'd tried to seduce him, subtly, gently, as a well-bred woman would do. When nothing of it worked, she resorted to shrewd means, fits of hysteria and cries that would raise the dead and provoke contrite feelings in the impenitent. She metamorphosed into infinite shapes and colors, but none of them seem to please the immutable man in front of her; whoever hasn't tried by all means to reach the object of their desire, even to the point of sacrificing their own selves for it, doesn't know how she felt. Miguel had a slight idea of the abyss that loomed in her mind; the imperative anguish that Sartre would call existentialist, which he just called volitional. For there's only anguish when there's volition, and if human beings were incapable of restraining their volition, then it'd be better to become cows or butterflies, infinitely less volitional and infinitely happier. Why, if Sartre is right, would anguish be man's privilege? The privilege of being enslaved to their circumstances. A wolf that kills its prey doesn't feel pity or remorse; it's necessary for him to kill. Why should Miguel feel any remorse for having done what was an urgent necessity? He had deliberated on his decision, but whatever course of action he had decided to take, he would have taken it out of mere necessity. Despite the fact that there had been millions of possibilities, from the moment he'd acted, that action had become a necessity, a product of his spiritual effort and his circumstances. Even the influence of a cloudy day, a delayed tram or piercing cold had been necessary to his decision. Everything had plotted that decision in its current shape and in every single detail. Nothing had been left to chance; his decision had been the most perfect and deliberate one.

112

"What now?" he thought. Someone had walked up to him at the entrance of a shopping center. He was asking him for money for food. "How much money does it take to eat?" he thought, "six zloty should be enough." But then, how much money did he want to give away? Was he feeling satisfied or grateful with life at the moment? He wasn't harboring any of those generous feelings; he gave him some groszy he had so as to make him leave him alone with his thoughts. He couldn't be bothered about worldly matters right now; he had inner problems to solve. He went back the same way he'd come; he was so lost in thoughts that he was afraid he'd lose his way if he tried to improvise his way back. How many times had he missed his stop because he read on the tram? But walking was different; he never got lost when he walked. It's true that he was disoriented, but provided he knew the streets, he never got lost. Coming back home was so full of connotations at the moment; he was retracing his steps just as he'd done with Luiza, returning to the starting point. Wasn't life just a game? Wasn't he just as good a player as he'd learnt to be? He'd lost that game with Luiza at least, and he knew he'd lost it because he knew it was over.

You're not ready, my heart
to desire what's due to you,
you fumble among your belongings
with a twitch of discontent,
you're not ready, my heart
to bear the ignominies of love
without relenting in your way
without despairing loneliness,
you're not ready my heart
and let it be your mea culpa,
whenever you're betrayed
for expecting the unexpectable,

I'm not ready, I'm not ready,

let it be your daily prayer

in your pursuit of freedom

from your vain desires.


## Chapter 33: One hundred years of solitude

*"There are four kinds of countries in the world: developed countries, undeveloped countries, Japan and Argentina."*- Simon Kuznets.

In 1946, Juan Domingo Peron was expanding the social welfare system and the secondary technical school system in Argentina. His idea was to create an industrialized economy based on a corporative system revolving around a strong state. He created a whole system of unions, nationalized public services and engaged in numerous public works. The country that had been one the richest in the world before the First World War had seen its wealth considerably reduced due to the global crisis in the thirties. A period of boom had allowed Peron to take advantage of people's optimism to bolster his populist regime. Everything was done not for the sake of the country, but for the mere love of power. The national bank had been nationalized in order to take loans to finance public expenditure. The only way to redemption, recognized a century before by Domingo Sarmiento, had been left aside. Holistic education, the key to social development, had been disregarded to make space for technocratic policies. An illiterate working class was handed the future of the country; they would haul the country into prosperity with the brute animal force they had been born with.

Sixty years later, after several coup d'états, ten years of radical liberalism and the greatest sovereign default in history, the country wasn't doing any better. New nationalistic measures were taken; a Spanish oil company was expropriated; there were restrictions on imports and on currency exchange. The current president was bracing herself for a new default, although this time not of the country's own making. The liberal global market didn't seem so liberal after all. Every possible dollar was being extracted from Argentina, with accumulated interest. The president's late husband had reached an agreement with the conscientious creditors that sought a compassionate solution to the problem, but there were always those keen on savage liberalism, who believed they had the right to trample on nations.

Argentina had lived through almost one hundred years of solitude, which had lasted since the decline of its golden period in 1917. It was 2015, two years short of the centennial of this lonely path Argentina had taken. However, looking at the demography of this country, it's not strange that it was not better developed; in general, South American countries were not doing that well economy wise. Argentina had come back to its roots after trying to stand out from the rest. This maneuver had gained the country the animosity of its neighbors, who rejoiced in Argentina's misfortunes until the country became humble again. Now Argentina was thinking about South American blocks and Chinese allies, when decades before it had walked hand in hand with the States. Now Argentina was denouncing the economic terrorism of the imperialist global power, but only because it had been seriously harmed by it. The political system had a history of corruption and demagogy which it needed to leave behind if the country was going to come back from its isolation. A new air started to be breathed as elections came near. The current president had already shown her true colors, after having bravely fought off the foreign vultures and the internal traitors. But no politician is exempt from corruption for long; the same system demands it and to be in power means to compromise. She had remained as faultless as possible, but she was losing popular support and it didn't seem that the many issues of the country were going to be solved soon.

That was the current situation in that large country. The currency had been devalued nine times since 2001. People were talking even more loudly about inflation and devaluation being the result of institutionalized fraud.

Argentina is the best example of economic mismanagement and all other countries try to learn from its mistakes so as not to follow suit. With some luck, it will one day escape from the cycle of getting out of a crisis just to enjoy a new decade of prosperity and then falling back again into semi-poverty.

## Chapter 34

Miguel had a recurrent nightmare in which he was fired from his job, he couldn't find a new one and he was forced to go back to Argentina. It wasn't success that he was looking for; he felt he'd be able to do what it takes to stay in Poland, even working eight hours a day for a corporation, sacrificing his intellect and creativity to the Green Bucks God. He knew that life was all about decisions and compromises. If he wanted to be able to support a family, he'd have to find a stable job and that per se would kill his creative drive. On the other hand, if he dedicated his life to writing, there'd be a moment when he'd dry up and his words would convey no meaning because he wasn't attached to reality anymore. He knew he should dedicate his life to living and writing as a means of expiation for his mistakes. "Success is a drug," he thought, "it doesn't change anything; it just numbs our consciousness so we don't feel the pain."

He spent a whole Saturday morning thinking of Luiza while he tried to ingest some literature. He wasn't able to focus on what he was reading; images of scenes with her crossed his inadvertent mind and took over his consciousness. "Why had she taken it so seriously?" he asked himself sadly. "Life is a game after all and no one knows all the rules. We were just playing together and I decided to draw back from the game. Why would she try to make it so difficult for us both to go on? Why wasn't she better

116

adapted to life and its vicissitudes?" But all those questions just filled him with bitterness. Then he thought of Hellen, the carefree wanderer of his nighttime fantasies. She was the opposite of Luiza and at the same time so similar. Both of them missed something; both of them failed to grasp life in its full meaning. However, it wasn't his job to bring Luiza back to the game; that match was over for him. He'd try to tame Hellen's heart and draw closer to her, without scaring her away. He'd texted her and she'd happened to be in the mood to answer him. They had a date the following day and he was planning on being gentle but firm, showing her his unequivocal intentions to bind his life to hers.

The D Day hour came and they met in a cafe downtown. It was six pm, rather early for a date, but he was planning on being resounding; he wanted a landslide victory, and small details didn't matter to him. She was smartly dressed, as for an evening occasion, and he was elegantly dressed too, which in daylight gave him the air of a Colombian drug dealer. However, the sun didn't make itself wait too long before setting behind the colorful buildings of Stary Rynek. She was radiant as usual and playfully malevolent as usual. He took on a sarcastic tone whenever he was with her although he always talked from the heart. She, however, seemed to hide herself behind her words, misguiding her interlocutor and letting him make his own conclusions about what she said. Miguel was at a loss by the end of the conversation; he didn't know whether she was interested or not; up to now it was a draw and he didn't know how to untie the game. He went for the obvious move; he invited her to dance. To his dismay, she accepted the offer. He liked that courage, so different from the reluctance of most girls. She assumed her role and played it, without hesitation. She seemed to be ahead of him in each of her moves, like a chess player that knows where she's leading her opponent. Miguel wasn't afraid to lose; he was just concerned about how much strain the game would exert on him.

Next she pulled out her phone and checked the time. It was a magical moment for Miguel because she had a normal cell phone, one of those which are meant only to communicate with people; no fancy Smartphone or iPhone was being held in her hands, but a simple cell phone, whose functions didn't go beyond calls, texting and an alarm sufficiently annoying to make sure she'd wake up on time. This anachronism suited her general disdain; he had a smartphone himself and he felt so little beside her. Miguel felt the urge to take the hand in which she held the phone and tell her: "I feel I could love you forever", but he checked this rush of emotion and contented himself with staring at her fingers while she put her phone back into her pocket.

"We can go now," she said, and as she stood up and walked away from the cafe table, he was dragged after her by her rare magnetism.

## Chapter 35

When he woke up the next morning, Hellen was already gone. He felt like he was in an American movie, only that he wasn't American and there was nothing fancy about the setting. The violence of this feeling woke him up from the lethargic state into which his mind had fallen while lying beside Hellen, and he reacted with all his might, but aimlessly. He didn't know what to do, whether to call her, to try to calm down or to try to put it all on paper. He was fumbling for reasons why she could've left without telling him, when he saw a message on his cell phone: "Sorry I left, I need to do some shopping."

He felt like smiling when he thought of the irony of such a trivial message vanquishing all his fears. "She's gone shopping, for goodness' sake," he repeated to himself. "Where will this girl lead me?"

He made some breakfast while uncalled-for images of the previous night rushed at him in disorderly succession. The first images to appear were of her pale nakedness and her blue eyes inciting him, spurring him to action.

She'd become eyes and hips, eyes and legs entwining and tightening around him, with a blotch of red lips interspersed all around. Then she'd become a tangle of dark brown hair that impregnated him with its rustic aroma while he rested his face on the pillow and nestled his nose among the waves of darkness. She'd also become that small belly he wrapped with his hand, as if hatching the fruit of his wildness. She'd also become those cold feet that sought the warmth of his and her tacit happiness, exuded by the motionlessness of her body in his arms.

Was he happy at that moment? How to define happiness when you're feeling it? It was a mixture of fear and hope; an infinite whole in his chest; a whole that could contain everything, but at the same time lacked everything. It was thirst; his happiness was infinite thirst, a thirst he didn't want to quench. What was he going to do then? Just try to put it aside for a moment to carry on with what earthlings call "life". He had some stuff to do that day and the sooner he started, the earlier he could get back to his reveries. Petty matters appeared even pettier in contrast with the feeling of immensity overpowering him. He felt like God must feel when listening to someone's enumeration of their trivial sins in the confessional. But he needed to get a grip of his emotions and put up with worldliness in spite of his desire to shout at every moment: "She's mine, she's mine and I love her all the more for that!"

Now whenever he saw a pretty girl or thought of one, they would all converge into Hellen. He would fancy many girls and gloat over fantasies with them just to end up with Hellen's eyes in front of him, beckoning him, alluring him with their reticence. He wasn't sure where her charm lay, whether in her beauty or in the way she managed it, but he wasn't too eager to break the spell.

**Chapter 36**

Miguel's following months were frantic. Hellen wasn't much into reading, but she was the literature Miguel had been looking for. They met often enough to keep the flame of their passion glowing, but not often enough to change each other's lives. For Miguel it was the perfect deal; he had enough of her in a weekly meeting. He could desire her for the rest of the week, building an alter image of her in his mind. Because in his fantasies, she was everything he desired and she wanted the same things as he did. Miguel was an inveterate naturalist so he believed that everyone has the same goals in life and that mere vanity impels people to differentiate themselves from others. He knew he wanted to have a family, and to age with a nice woman beside him and children around him. He knew that every sensible woman wanted the same, but that there were other factors that also influenced their decisions. Sometimes people sacrifice their natural right of procreation to a higher way of love, love for everyone in general and no one in particular. But sometimes people may just be too dejected to be able to plan on happiness; they just see what's in front of them so they'd rather have instant pleasure than a long-lasting burden. Hellen was in the second situation, although she wanted to believe she was in the first one. As a soul with artistic propensities, but with a dim intellect, she aspired to artificiality in art, which she mistook for sublimity. Her love of art for art's sake made her contemptuous towards essential things like cooking or taking care of someone else's feelings. She believed that art was liberating, so she was honestly deceiving herself whenever she put all her energies into her profession and left no remnant of enthusiasm or patience to deal with Miguel's moody character. Whenever he showed that he was upset or down, she'd just let it go away by itself and she'd come back when he was in a state in which they could have a pleasant time together.

Miguel, in contrast, was always available to her. He took her aloofness, her rejection and her selfishness as part of the karmic deal he'd probably made in a previous life. He knew he was in love with her, so why question her moral qualities? Whether she was good or bad to him, it didn't matter; he only knew that she was what his spirit was yearning for. She was beyond good and evil to him; she was just necessary.

Thus the relationship went on for months. Miguel would offset his lack of emotional fulfillment by writing and Hellen would just not take Miguel's tantrums seriously. Miguel hoped Hellen would grow out of her sentimental torpor and Hellen would just systematically overlook all of Miguel's fits of passion. She had managed to keep their relationship casual for almost two years and Miguel's mood swings had gradually stopped, giving place to a more sedate kind of affection. Everything else was sublimated in the pages of his books, which grew thicker and thicker, bloated by his inner rebellions and occasional daily nightmares.

His friend Steven had gone back to the States, so his spiritual inquisitiveness gave way to a more settled attitude of accepting of his lot. He knew he was always in control of his life, that it was up to him to change the chain of events that made up his destiny, but at the moment he was content with his life. He was happy because he thought he was.

## Chapter 37

It was something gradual and he couldn't tell for sure when he'd started being dishonest with himself. He started looking for means of diversion from his own life. He wanted out, at least for a moment, at least once a day. He'd started looking at other girls with more desire than he had for Hellen. He remembered that when he'd broken up with Luiza, he'd had many nightmares and woken up several times with tears in his eyes. Now, in contrast, he was having daily nightmares because of being with Hellen. Life looked transient again and everything became relative. He could be with Hellen, but he could just as easily have been with someone else; there was no substantial difference for him. Because love is a construct and we decide on its value. Hellen, as an artist prone to romantic ideals, believed in soul mates and had many times hinted that Miguel could be her other half. Miguel had never taken his cue and he had just let the moment pass and fade away inconsequentially. For Miguel, love was something unutterable; it wasn't a formula that leads you to someone, but rather a power that liberates you from your emotional bonds. For him to talk of love was to talk of detachment and not of a romantic quest for our other selves. He was sure he didn't love Hellen and he was becoming increasingly sure that he never would do. It was just impossible to love someone whom he didn't feel grateful to.

He still desired her, for she was always sexy, especially when she was close to him, but after, when they were apart, he felt she was alien to him; her splendid beauty was transformed into a grotesque caricature which he couldn't chase away from his mind. In the end, he told her he wasn't in love with her anymore and she took it dramatically well, which showed him she hadn't given a thought to their relationship before. In breakups sometimes we realize what the other person's feelings are, even when this person has been too reserved or too proud to tell us. But in this case, there were simply no feelings on Hellen's part. She analyzed the news so as to know how the new situation would affect her, but nothing more happened inside her at the time.

## Chapter 38

Britain had recently announced that it would beef up its defenses in the Falkland Islands. The current Argentinean president, Cristina de Kirschner, was a populist leader and she also had the propensity to fight to the death for lost causes, as the Che Guevara had done. Let's not confuse dying for a cause with killing for a cause. The current English prime minister, David Cameron, would surely kill for his cause, and he was just making provisions for a second war over the Falklands.

The funny thing was that Cameron was blaming the militarization of the Falklands on Argentina, maybe because he saw the ghosts of Argentinean dictators raising from their tombs or an eighty year-old former junta general taking power in a currently democratic country, taking a new loan from the IMF in order to militarize the country, making the opposition disappear and invading the Falklands again in a final act of despotism to glorify his great regime. The thing is Cameron only knew the law of the sword, and in his mind an argument could only be solved by muscle flexing and an eventual fight.

Cristina, in a response that showed why women are better heads of states than men, told Cameron to spend his pounds on food for his people instead of armaments; she told him: "We aren't a threat to you." And anyone who'd ever heard their discourses had probably felt the difference between a person who, although seldom brilliant and many times even plainly ridiculous, speaks up for her ideals and a kid who'd probably go to war against Putin just for the sake of playing tin soldiers on a big scale. The truth is that Argentina has been in no position to invade anyone since the end of the dictatorship. The country has been greatly demilitarized, for imagine how happy Argentinians would be if after defaulting to other countries and its own people, the country still kept its warships. As Cristina said: "Going to war wasn't the decision of a democratic government," so the Argentinian nation can't be held accountable for that. But, as people who haven't learned much about life always believe that fighting for something implies destroying an enemy, Cameron was just being judicious when he decided to make an outpost out of a small colony. He didn't know that the Falklands were an Argentinian ideal, a dream Argentinians liked to think about to forget that the world has been built by conquerors. They wanted the Falklands as Indians want their land, just to contemplate it and take pride in it; they had no intention to go and settle in one of the coolest regions on Earth, and the oil and fish companies would probably be foreign-owned anyway, as are most of Argentina's industries.

## Chapter 39

Hellen was an idealist. In her mind, there was no excuse for Miguel having told her that he wasn't in love anymore. She didn't feel in love either and many times she found herself unconsciously flirting with other men, but she always managed to give no consequence to everything that wasn't deliberately done. Therefore, when she heard him say those drastic words, she did not try to relate to him. She just despised him all the more because she had the same feelings, but she'd been discreet enough not to be aware of them herself.

She left him the following day; she just needed one afternoon to get over a two-and-a-half-year relationship. She was an idealist; she believed that one love fades away and a new one emerges; she knew that love was waiting for her on the corner of some street and she needed to go. So she left; she didn't make any trouble about material things. The stuff she needed, she carried to her mother's on a friend's truck; the rest she left to Miguel. No tears were dropped over meaningless things; she didn't even stop for a second when she crossed the threshold which she'd never step over again. Years later, thoughts of Miguel would come to her mind as in a revery or a movie she'd seen long ago. But in all these images, he'd never again reject her or dump her; he'd just be a sad character who played a secondary role in her life.

## Chapter 40: On capital punishment

Is it me or is capital punishment the symptom of a society that's too attached to life? Because the general debate when touching this issue is about the respect for life and whether we, as human beings, have the right to take a life, or whether we're transgressing the rights of nature or of

God. This debate is also important, but it's also out of focus. Because the point is not to know whether we have the right to kill or not; the point is to know whether we're issuing the right sentence. Because, in my view, a person who kills will be killed, because that's the law of nature. But the issue should be whether we have the capacity or rather the omniscience to judge fairly. And to this question I answer "No, never". When did we start thinking that we can replace God or Nature in their omniscience? How can we think that we can replace the law of cause and effect? Because, if we're killing a man to save us trouble, to put him out of service, to switch him off so he won't harm other people, in that case, capital punishment works, but if we're thinking that we're doing a good to humanity, we're wrong; we're as wrong as we would be by thinking that killing an enemy in a war is doing a good to humanity. I won't promote martyrdom here because very few of us are ready to die, but I'll just say that dying is, in humanistic terms, better than killing. Having said that, who's ready to give up his life to improve humanity? So we're in an impasse right now and that's why we kill murderers and the enemy, because we're afraid of dying. So I think that capital punishment doesn't have much to do with respect for life, because people in favor of capital punishment may respect life more than people against it. Again, people in favor of capital punishment may be more religious than people against it, but they may choose to decide that God didn't write the sixth commandment or they may just forget that karmic law is inevitable. Capital punishment has to do more with fear for our own lives than with moral concerns. We kill so as not to be killed, as simple as that. Disguise it under all the moral reasons you want, but you'll never get over this simple axiom: by destroying the enemy we always hope to put an end to a problem. That's the idea behind wars: all wars are the war to end all wars. And that's the idea behind punishment: we're harming you so you won't harm us anymore.

The problem is that when we see an evil act, we just see the human injustice of it, but we don't see the divine justice. When we see a man that is a mass murderer or when we see the enemy's threatening face, we just think of the injustice they committed or want to commit and we don't see any divine law behind it. Fear is like any narcotic; it blinds us and doesn't allow us to see beyond the present moment. We must always try to keep in mind that everything that happens to us is deserved. So, if we're victims of a war or if we have suffered an injury, it's always just. The same goes for murdered people. We can only see the human injustice of a guy who woke up one day, went to a school and shot down random people. We can't see the divine justice behind it; our fear blinds us. I won't become an advocate of murderers here and I won't try to dismantle an institution as old as society: prison, or try to promote the liberation of murderers. I don't believe murderers should be let free; the only thing I disagree with is the humanization of law. Law has always been and will always be divine and therefore human laws are just etiquette rules for society and not moral standards. What I want to say here is that we're imprisoning people out of fear and we're killing them because we're too attached to our lives. As simple as that. So we should start rethinking the judicial system and our foreign policies and thinking twice before fighting terrorism with guns.

## Chapter 41

He appreciated Hellen more than ever now that she was gone. Now his desire for her became a positive thing; now it really hurt. Now that she was gone, he liked her more; now her romanticism and idealism filled the house with sweet aromas and made him feel her full absence. What was he going to do now? Now that he was free. He hadn't planned on being free; now his troubles started. Now he needed to take the reins of his life again. What suddenly struck him was that it had been more than two years since he'd last seen or heard about Luiza. He'd forgotten her for all this time and now the yearning for her surged from his guts with the same impetus of a repressed nation that's just been waiting for its chance of revolution. He'd lost every right to even talk to her by now, but his romanticism was superior to his attentiveness and consideration. He knew that in that heart he'd neglected there would always be a place for him. He didn't know what he wanted from Luiza; he just knew that he wanted to see her now that his life was revolutionized. He wanted to extrapolate his present incertitude from his past feelings for Luiza, which had seemed so solid to him back then.

Miguel knew nothing about Luiza's current life because she was a discrete person and she never put anything personal on Facebook. From her sporadic posts he knew that she'd been on a journey to Rome a couple of months ago, that she still liked Chopin and that she was as religious as ever. He checked all her posts once again, looking for some clue to her present life, but he couldn't find anything substantial. She seemed to be doing well; that was the impression he'd always had of her whenever he saw one of her posts. That was what he wanted to hear and he hadn't inquired any further. But now he wanted to make sure she was fine. Out of his own need to be fine he wanted her to be fine too. It was as if the only thing he needed at that moment was to know she was happy.

He still had her phone number in his contact list. He stared at the cyphers asking them tacitly about the whereabouts of their owner. Was she still living in Poznan? Had she been carried away by life's constant flow? Could he even attempt to reach her at that moment? He knew only that at that moment there was no other goal in his life than to find her and see her smile. He was aware that he'd regressed to his dependence on her because he needed some lightening up, but he didn't mind a little help at that critical moment of his life.

At first he wanted to text her, but he gave up on this idea. He didn't know what to write; everything sounded comical to him. What would he say? Hello, it's me, Miguel, the guy who wants to check on you now that he has nothing better to do with his life? Would he send her a message jammed with words to which she wouldn't be able to find any appropriate response? No, he knew women and he knew himself; and above all he knew that the combination of women's coyness and his verbosity was hopeless. So he decided to call her. At least in that way he'd have the upper hand; she'd be baffled by his call and he'd be able to say anything that came to his mind because she'd be too focused on her emotions to pay any attention to what was being said. In this way he'd also get an honest response from her, a spontaneous and heartrending response.

It was 7 pm and he had no excuse not to call her, so he did. The phone rang four times before she answered, only four times. He would've waited a thousand rings to hear her voice; the fact of learning that he'd always been only four rings away from her almost broke his heart. A monomaniacal thought crossed his mind: "She's always been ready to answer my call. She's been waiting for it for two years and a half." The thought left him speechless. What to say now? Would it be possible to apologize now? "Sorry I didn't call you for two years and a half" would be too humiliating for her; it even sounded like a joke when he rehearsed it in his mind. But he hadn't spoken for three seconds and the situation was becoming tenser. She hadn't said a word either, except a faint "hello" that expressed anguish, excitement and expectation all at once. He was painful to her; he didn't need to resort to his sensitiveness to realize it. If he'd had any control over his actions, he would've hung up on her and let her be and let her recover from him once and for all. But he'd smelled blood and he couldn't stop himself from wanting to achieve the kill. He was in the game and now he wouldn't abandon it until he was defeated.

"Hello", he said, and then he blurted, "How're you Luiza? I'm sorry to call without warning."

"I'm OK thanks and you?" she said reflexively.

"Fine Luiza, I've just broken up with Hellen." He wasn't sure if Luiza knew about Hellen; he knew those weren't the nicest words to say to a person who had been deeply in love with you after two and a half years of silence. But he couldn't check himself and he preferred to let his words blurt out of his mouth; everything he said was as astonishing to him as it was to her.

"I'm sorry for you," she said in a way that effaced everything but the fact that he was suffering. She'd snuffed out her emotions and quietened her feelings to be able to be there for him at that moment. She'd forgiven him a thousand times already for not having called, for disappearing from her life, for having abandoned her, for making promises he wouldn't fulfill. She was above rancor, beyond rage and disappointment. She was just a kindred soul helping him.

"Luiza... I'd like to see you," he said. "Do you think you have some free time?"

She had a moment's hesitation that he misinterpreted. He thought that she was struggling inside; that she couldn't reconcile her feelings. He didn't have any idea that she was only worried about him; she was trying to find the way to tell him something she felt he must know.

"Yes", she said. "We can meet tomorrow around 6 pm. Is that OK for you?"

"Yes. Where?"

"Let's meet in front of the fountain in Plac Wolnosci," she said.

"OK, see you then," he answered automatically. And he waited for three seconds before hanging up. It was too strenuous for him to try to build a sentence at that moment.


## Chapter 42: A theory of jokes

Why do we laugh? Aristotle and Plato would say that it's triggered by the pleasure derived from seeing someone else's defects or even our own defects. Thus we feel superior to the person we're laughing at, even if it's ourselves. This theory doesn't account, however, for children's laughter, because they don't laugh out of a feeling of superiority. Other philosophers, like Francis Hutcheson and Kant, were more inclined towards the idea that we laugh at the perception of the incongruity of a situation or that we laugh when our expectations are transformed into nothing. This is an interesting theory, but it doesn't account for laughing from tickles, where there's no time for perception or for building expectations. Other theories could be named, just for the sake of thoroughness, although they don't contribute anything new. That's the case with Henri Bergson's theory of social adaptation, where laughter is a side effect. "Laughter is the eruption of emotions repressed by society," he says, and he's right in a way, but he's not as insightful as Freud is in matters of repression. George Vaillant also proposed that jokes are a defense mechanism, a way of avoiding confrontation, which doesn't account for linguistic jokes and misinterprets the act of making fun of something, which is not a way of avoiding confrontation but an actual way of expression; if Valliant were right then all kinds of art would be a defense mechanism.

The only theory that accounts for all aspects of laughter is Freud's relief theory. This theory originated with Spencer, who said that laughter is an economical phenomenon. Then Freud explained that jokes are an emotional shortcut by which we find a rapid solution to an emotional problem. This sudden relief of an emotional burden provokes pleasure, which in turn provokes laughter. Then laughter is just a reflex action, a reaction to pleasure. That accounts for children laughing when they are stimulated and people laughing from tickles, which is just a way of releasing the tension provoked by the tickles.

Therefore, we must differentiate jokes from humor. Jokes are a construct, an artificial way of provoking laughter, while humor is our natural predisposition to be surprised by the world or to take pleasure in what we do. Thus, humor is indispensable for jokes because no joke can stimulate a numb mind.

We can create a categorization of jokes according to their comic methods or comic effects:

The first method could be called Incongruity, which was the way in which the Greek philosophers used believe all jokes work. Incongruous jokes are those that provoke a change in our mental framework by presenting us with a novel way to deal with a situation. The discovery of this simpler perspective provokes pleasure in us. For example, two friends were talking in a bar: "Marriage scares me." "Why?" "Because according to the statistics, fifty percent of marriages end up lasting forever."

The second method is called Puns. This method is easy to explain; when a word has two meanings and we exploit its full potential, we provoke mental economy, which produces pleasure. For instance: what does a fish say when it hits its head against the fishbowl? Dam!

Analogy is the third method, which consists of finding a similarity between two ideas that are apparently disconnected. Like in the case of Puns and Incongruity, this discovery provokes mental economy and therefore pleasure. For instance: we should learn from the weather; it pays no heed to criticism.

The fourth method is called Hyperbole and consists of exaggerating something until it becomes ridiculous. When this thing or idea is ridiculed, there's an automatic relief of all the tension associated with it. Hyperbole works, therefore, only with serious topics, like death and religion; for instance, the joke about Pope Francis who, at an airport, was awaited by a limousine to carry him to his residence. He stood beside the driver's door and wouldn't budge, so the chauffeur asked him to please sit on the back seat, to which the Pope answered: "The only way I'll get into this car is if I drive." The chauffeur was distraught and he wished he hadn't gone to work that day; to his entreaties and his arguments about losing his job the Pope simply answered: "And who will know? This will remain only between you, me and God." The chauffeur sat down and thought nothing could be worse, until he was proven wrong by the Pope; he jammed down the accelerator and they sped along at up to a hundred miles per hour. A few minutes later they heard sirens and the Pope pulled up. When the policeman saw who was driving he went back to his car and called his superior: "Sir, I have an issue. I've stopped a limousine for speeding, but inside there's a very important person." "Who is it? The governor?" asked the chief. "More important," said the policeman. "The president then?" "More important." "So who the hell is he?!" "I think it's God" "Are you out of your mind?! Why do you think it's God?" "Because the Pope is chauffeuring him."

The last method is called Tendency. This method works in the same way as Hyperbole, except it focuses on someone or something specific rather than ideas in general. By hearing or telling tendentious jokes, we release the hatred or contempt we feel for a certain thing or person.

This last method betrays our values and prejudices. A churchgoer will be less inclined to laugh at a joke about the Church, because their mechanism of criticism is smothered by their social needs. In general, independent or solitary persons are more inclined to comedy. We can mention, for instance, a joke about Obama: what technique does Obama use to sleep? First he lies on one side then he turns to the other.

## Chapter 43

What happened that afternoon seemed like life was playing a practical joke on him. He was already upset because she hadn't invited him to her place; she'd chosen a public stage for their drama. He'd thought that she was too shy to invite him to her home after so much time apart, but when he asked her why she hadn't invited him home he was taken aback by her answer. She told him she couldn't invite him home because she hadn't had the courage to tell Alonso about him.

"Alonso?" He asked, in a way which was more ironic than surprised, as if he was not actually surprised by the fact that she had a new boyfriend but by the fact that he had a fancy name, just like one out of a South American soap opera.

"I met him a year ago", she said, but there was something her eyes said, although her lips were quiet.

"What? He asked in an impatient tone, which he switched for a more empathetic one. "What happened?" he asked again.

"I'm two months pregnant," she said and her face suddenly lightened up. It was as if she'd uttered magic words that changed her mood and filled her with an inner glow. Miguel just stared at her in contemplation. He wasn't happy or sad, so why say anything? He was mesmerized by a new shade in her eyes, a more radiant one.

"That's great," he said, meaning the new shade in her eyes rather than her pregnancy.

"I'm so happy," she said. "And now that I see you and I can share this with you, I'm just... I'm so glad to see you." She said, as if trying to check a rush of emotions from overwhelming her. When Miguel realized that she couldn't utter another word, he went on.

"So this Alonso, what's he like? Is he Spanish?"

"Yes," she said. "He's Spanish. He came to Poznan two years ago. He's very nice to me and he's so in love with me and I ... I love him so much."

"I'm very happy, Luiza. I'm happy you found what you were looking for."

"I had stopped looking for it after you," she said confessionally, "but when I met him I started believing in happiness again."

They started walking somewhere and nowhere, as if trying to avoid passiveness. Both of them were full of emotions and they both could only submit to the circumstances, but they wanted to rebel at least

133

symbolically so they escaped from a situation which, however, followed them everywhere. They crossed a bridge and saw the Varta River flowing indifferently beneath them; its waters ran as profusely as their feelings. They talked of nothing, of a book he'd read, of a new project of the Church she was into; they disputed about religious and moral issues as if they were two political enemies or hooligans from different football teams. After half an hour of heated discussion, they realized that they hadn't lost that habit.

In the end they arrived at the point of departure; they were back to Stary Rynek and it was getting late. She said that she had to go home, but that he should come over some day. He promised to visit her and to be kind to Alonso; even though he didn't pin much hope on a man with such a name. She just smiled her knowing smile and then made the playful grimace of contempt with which she always welcomed Miguel's jokes, so as never to allow him the pride of making her laugh. But he only grew more animated whenever she pretended not to appreciate his jokes, so he went on:

"I see he's already given you a ring. I've just noticed it. I thought you were just wearing an item from your diamond jewelry collection."

"So funny," she said, "but you're right. It has a small diamond in it."

"I know; you must have done the same as Laura Ingalls."

"Who?"

"Laura Ingalls, a girl whose boyfriend asked her whether she'd like an engagement ring; to which she answered that it would depend on who gave her the ring. And when he said that it was he who wanted to give her the ring, she answered: then it would depend on the ring."

"OK, you're past funny," she said, but she only drew up the corners of her lips slightly, as if in a deliberate effort to put up with his jokes. He knew he couldn't expect more from a person whose only aim in life had been to ensnare him in her love webs; he knew she was used to effacing herself in front of him to the point of not desiring or enjoying anything but his company. He knew she was merry just because he was merry, and this was not in the least related to the humorous quality of his jokes. So he dropped the stand-up comedy and resigned himself to being a simple display item for Luiza, which meant that nothing he could do would diminish or augment her interest in him and that there would always be a sparkle in her eyes whenever he was around.

He walked her to her house, like in the old times, and he left her in the safety of the life she'd built with love and care. He was happy to take part in her happiness.

## Chapter 44: A story of two men

There were two brothers who were born in a well-off family. Their parents provided them with all they needed to do well in life. They had a good education and their parents' support. When they grew up, they took different paths. The elder brother wanted to make his parents proud, so he studied medicine and graduated with honors. The younger one wasn't sure about what he wanted in life so he stayed longer at his parents' trying to find an occupation that could suit him. In the end, he finished his studies although he knew that a degree wasn't anything meaningful to him.

Years passed and both brothers found a job. The elder brother found a job as director of a hospital and the younger one found odd jobs that nevertheless allowed him to get by. Every evening both of them sat in the solitude of their respective apartments and they enjoyed their free time. Both of them dedicated themselves to what gave them pleasure, various things, from reading to watching a video, from visiting friends to simply going for a walk. Both of them also had a habit that they invariably followed every day. For fifteen minutes the elder brother would think of all his achievements and take pride in them. Sometimes he'd write them down on a piece of paper; sometimes he'd just list them in his head. The younger brother would also invariably consume fifteen minutes of his life, but not by counting his achievements, that wouldn't have taken him that long; instead he'd grab one of the oranges he bought regularly at the market, peel it and it eat it with genuine delight.

More years passed and both brothers got married to good women and had kids. The elder brother could afford to provide the best environment and the best education for his children, but the younger one also found a way. Although he didn't earn much, he prioritized his children so they never lacked anything they needed.

More years passed and both brothers became grandpas and were retired. Now they had all the time in the world to do what gave them pleasure. No matter what they did, they'd always keep up their respective habits. The elder one would always count all his personal achievements, a task that took him almost an hour by now. The younger one would spend almost an hour eating oranges, but because he wasn't as hurried as when he was young, he could take as long as he liked to eat just one orange.

More years passed and both brothers got ill. They were lying on their respective deathbeds surrounded by their loved ones. Both of them were happy; they'd lived a full life and they were surrounded by love. However, there was a small difference between them. When the elder brother tried to give some meaning to his life, he sought for it among the things he'd always done, among his habits. He realized then that he'd always spent some minutes of the day listing all of his achievements. But now that he was leaving this world, that activity looked ludicrous to him: "Vainly have I spent all those minutes of my life," he said, "when the reality is that all my personal achievements will die with me." And a tear of sadness ran down his cheek. When the younger brother tried to find a meaning to his life, he did the same as his brother; he looked among his habits and he found out he'd been eating oranges daily since he could remember. But in contrast to his brother, this didn't sadden him; on the contrary, he

136

thought: "Oranges are such delicious fruits; I'm happy I ate so many of them." And a beam of happiness spread on his face.

## Chapter 45: Luiza

Two years and a half before, when Luiza at last understood that Miguel would never be ready to make a commitment to her, she felt sorry for both of them, but at the same moment she felt relieved of a heavy burden. Being in love with him was the right thing to do, her heart and her spirit told her, but it so strained her nerves and her psyche that she wasn't sure she'd be able to withstand it. She was a religious person, so she never yielded to pain; it was her highest pride: to suffer for someone she loved. She was by no means looking for a way out, but when she was freed from the bond she'd herself fastened to her spirit, she cried from disillusionment and relief.

At first, when their meetings started to dwindle to sporadic visits, Luiza couldn't help crying from despair. The death sentence that had been signed for their love was being slowly executed and she couldn't bear that sight. At first, she'd tried to rebel, to precipitate events so as to end the agony, but her efforts were in vain, because she was afraid of not seeing Miguel again as much as she was afraid of his getting emotionally detached from her. The things she'd thought she wouldn't be able to withstand became more bearable as they became more real. Months before she'd thought she'd die if she saw him beside another woman and now she'd barely twitched when she'd seen him walking hand in hand with someone. He'd seen her and he hadn't stopped; he'd walked by totally unaware of the revolution in her heart. She'd seen the empathy in his eyes, but also the resolution in his movements. He'd resolved to pass by her in spite of her feelings, in spite of their common past. A scene that could only have taken place in the worst of her nightmares had just been realized and she was relieved because she felt nothing worse could happen to her now.

For weeks she lay in a lethargic state, not finding a way out of her immobility, but at last she decided to force herself into happiness. After all, she was young and beautiful and she didn't want to waste the vital energy that ran through her veins and blossomed in her face and body. She went to a party in a new club. She'd been invited on Facebook and many acquaintances of hers were going. She was sure to have a good time if she could get out of her melancholy mood. She put on her best attire, a blue short linen scoop-neck dress with cap sleeves and decorative studding. She wasn't fond of makeup, but she decided to wear blue eyeliner to set off her eyes, as well as foundation with just a hint of blush, and fuchsia lipstick. For the first time in months, she saw her full beauty and while she admired herself in front of the mirror she forgot all her disappointment.

Although she knew some people at the party, she remained in a corner, watching people dance, too self-aware to enjoy herself. The few people who knew her exchanged a few words with her and then went on having fun, mindless of her inner struggle to breathe and keep calm. She was so deep in her thoughts that at first she paid no attention to a guy who was introducing himself to her. He was telling her for the second time "Hi, I'm Alonso, and you?" He was on the verge of leaving, abashed by her non-reaction, when she answered tenuously, "I'm Luiza, nice to meet you." However, she couldn't draw a smile on her face, in spite of the inviting beam on her interlocutor's face. But he seemed happy enough to have gotten a response from what he'd deemed a lost cause a second ago. He started asking personal questions, but he was so natural and kindhearted that she answered them gladly. His wide-open eyes were fixed on hers with a sort of magnetism she had seldom felt before. She felt she could order this guy to do anything and he'd do it gladly; she felt in control; she felt desired by a warm heart and that filled her with hopes.

He asked her if she wanted to dance and she assented with a reproachful gesture. She'd been waiting for him to ask her to dance and she'd grown a little restless as he dragged on the conversation. Now they were dancing and she was making full use of her sensuality. She let herself be embraced and led by him and whenever he gave her some freedom of movement, she turned around and let herself be embraced from behind, grabbing his hands as he placed them on her hips. The eroticism of the dance was the best remedy for the bitterness and regret from her past; at that moment she could only feel the present, which was palpitating and overwhelmingly vivid. She was drunk with pleasure and she manifested it in the gracefulness of her movements. Her dancing partner was obviously glad of her joyfulness and she was glad to make him glad. That stranger had surreptitiously become meaningful to her; he was the mirror in which her full beauty was reflected. Her life took on another hue in his presence; he was like the light that illuminates a flower.

## Chapter 46

It was two weeks before Luiza agreed to go on a date with Alonso. They didn't talk on Facebook because she didn't want the magic of their first encounter to be marred by the triviality of daily messaging. She believed that silence made part of the best symphonies and that space was needed for their feelings to grow healthily. When at last she agreed to meet him, she noticed she was as excited as a child that has been waiting for Christmas. It was a sweet sensation and she cherished it dearly. Alonso was a simple guy and he'd invited her simply to go for a drink and talk, but the charm of their second meeting lay exactly in its simplicity and spontaneity. She'd been afraid that their second encounter wouldn't match the expectations she'd built up during those two weeks.

Alonso had come from Spain a couple of years before and he had the affable temperament that characterizes Spaniards. He seemed to have not a worry in the world when he was with her; just to see him talk amiably and listen with attention to what she said could lead anyone to believe that Spain was doing better than Switzerland in economic matters and that the Spanish king gave all of his subjects an annuity of fifteen thousand Euros. There was an inherent optimism in his ways, but he never seemed to be joking; all the things he said, funny as they may have sounded, seemed to come directly from the heart, without being filtered by the self-defeating brain.

He told her he'd come to Poland because of the recession, but also because he found Polish girls unsettlingly beautiful. Once he'd seen such beauty he couldn't leave Poland anymore. "What about marrying a Polish girl and taking her back with you to Spain?" Luiza asked him in a joking tone.

"I don't know, would you like to?" he said, and this answer would've seemed offensively blunt were it not for the everlasting smile on his face. That smile was a balm to Luiza's disappointed heart; it assuaged her fears and gave her the strength to answer, although she didn't smile back: "Yes, I would like to. Whenever you're ready."

Alonso ceased fire for a second. He stopped smiling and examined carefully the casualties. He saw that no damage had been done, that she had just surrendered a stronghold to him and that this required solemnity on his part. He assented to her with his head and then, still looking at her, started smiling again, for no reason and without saying anything.

That night Luiza cried a double share of tears. She cried for her past disappointment and for her present happiness. She mourned her love for Miguel and welcomed her new love, which had taken the shape of Alonso. When she compared them both she saw contrasting colors; where Miguel had been melancholic and reticent, Alonso was cheerful and expansive. Miguel had made her question herself as well as many things in her life, while Alonso accepted everything as it was and seemed to be happy no matter what. She asked herself if it wasn't too early to give away her heart like that. After all, Alonso may just have been nice to her out of his natural kindness. Fears started to overpower her again and she decided to repress her feelings, to not give herself to joy yet. Now she just cried for Miguel, to forget and forgive him for what he'd done and to leave him behind so she could start anew.

## Chapter 47

Many days passed before Miguel could fulfill his promise to go and visit her. He thought that Alonso was as good as a person can be. Alonso either still didn't know about him or he was completely OK with an ex-boyfriend visiting his fiancée. During the whole hour they spent together not a single allusion to the past was made. Everything was focused on the present, with some hints about the future. Miguel couldn't stand it for more than one hour so he started saying goodbye after Alonso took his eyes off him for a couple of seconds.

During the meeting he'd noticed that she wasn't the same in front of Alonso. Her world didn't revolve around Miguel anymore. It seemed that she'd changed her axis and now she was rotating around Alonso. He liked the way she'd blossomed. It was so pleasant for him to see that her happiness didn't depend on him anymore; he felt very light now that he could just enjoy the spectacle of her radiance without the burden of having to perform in it.

However, among all the gladness, he could identify a feeling of jealousy that gave a sour touch to the sweetness of his current emotions. In some place in his heart he still wanted to be the suffering hero, the romantic character who sacrifices his life for a cause. He couldn't help feeling that Alonso's role belonged to him. It would've been easier if it really was a movie or a book rather than real life. Then he could get rid of an annoying character with two strokes of his pen. Stephen had told him once about a literary trick called Deus ex Machina, which consisted in resorting to a fatal event to solve a deadlocked situation. Maybe he could have Alonso die from badly treated pneumonia; maybe he could just have him run over by a bus in a frantic Spanish street intersection while visiting his family. The possibilities were innumerous. "If only it was a book," he thought mournfully. Or maybe he could kill him for real, but no, someone might find out; Alonso might not die a quiet death and he might give Miguel away, thus ruining his perfect plan to stab a knife into the back of his ribs. Besides, Alonso might move during the procedure or even turn, which would produce a front wound in the abdomen, which Miguel wanted to avoid: he hadn't been able to stand seeing stomach wounds since he'd had an abdominal operation years before. Yes, definitely, Alonso didn't look sensitive enough to allow for a dignified death; he'd surely protest or behave wildly while being stabbed, like a decapitated chicken running around headlessly. Miguel resigned himself to his lot. He knew the world would be a better place if unwanted people just died or got lost on deserted islands, but unfortunately things didn't adjust themselves to his ideals and reality had a stronger influence over life.

But then he thought if Alonso were hurt, Luiza would suffer. Miguel didn't want to deprive her of her happiness and she was happier than ever. So he'd have to resort to all his art to accept the situation and let Alonso live. Of course, in real life people died, but death is not the realm of art, only life is, and Miguel was an artist.


**Chapter 48**

She opened the door as she'd always done it: hiding herself behind it and not turning her face towards Miguel until she'd finished locking it. She lifted her gaze from the floor to Miguel's eyes and just then he recognized the same person he'd met three years ago. She had aged; the first wrinkles had started to appear on her face, signs of maturity and experience. But

142

her eyes carried a deeper meaning for him. Those were the same eyes; eyes he remembered from a long time ago, and in their unchangeable nature lay their profound meaning to Miguel. He saw his life in a three-second-long flashback; his whole life passed through his mind, starting with the day he first saw her. It was a party and they were full of youth. Then he saw his deathbed, a few years ahead, and he saw those eyes again, regarding him unrelentingly. Those eyes which, he was completely sure, would lose their glare and intensity only when he died; then and only then those eyes would unfix themselves from him and would shut and rest in peace.

"Where is Tommy?" He asked, as if conjuring up the only thing that existed between them, in a last effort not to succumb to the magnetism of her unquenchable love.

"He's with his father," she answered, and Miguel was disarmed of the last weapon he could use to try to fight an unwinnable battle. Tommy was the only setback she'd had in her maniacal battle for Miguel; everything else she'd done had been directed towards him. She'd started going out with Alonso to try to forget Miguel and she'd finally canceled the wedding with Alonso because she hadn't succeeded in driving Miguel from her heart. But when Tommy was born, she saw Miguel's place in her heart being challenged by a new contender. At first, this feeling dismayed her because she felt her heart would be smashed by this violent change, but then she saw that Tommy's and Miguel's presences, far from antagonizing each other, joined efforts to finally commingle into a harmonious whole that swelled her heart with joy.

Miguel could see that she was happy; her love for him had remained intact and her face wasn't contorted in anguish anymore. Now that she wasn't with him anymore, she could put all her energies into loving him, without having to deal with possessiveness and jealousy. Now those emotions couldn't reach her, since she'd given up her right to be a part of his life.

Now she wasn't upset by what he did because his actions were only his; it wasn't her responsibility anymore.

They talked about life though they didn't talk about themselves. They had experienced many things and, nevertheless, all that was irrelevant now. They had nothing to tell to each other; it was as if they'd left it off three years before and now they'd taken it up again, exactly at the same place. Nothing else mattered but their affair, their spiritual exchange that had been postponed for a while. Now they were mature enough to continue it; the inevitable was going to take place and they were going to free themselves from physical bonds and be happier in spite of themselves. When Miguel got up from the couch, he felt a heaviness in his whole body, as if an anchor had been hooked to his waist and he couldn't move so freely any longer. However, this anchor, far from deranging him, gave him the stability he was lacking. For in the sea of emotions he'd always experienced, many a time he'd blindly sought a harbor in which to rest his weariness, and now he felt he could weigh anchor and harbor himself anywhere. So he weighed it patiently, welcoming the new load, and bid Luiza goodbye for the time being, knowing that he'd never go astray again. But before he left, she asked him: "Why do you like me Miguel? Why are you here with me right now?"

"Because you're an interminable song by Chopin; you make me sad, but I can't stop listening," was his response.

He leaned towards her, always staring at her eyes. Their lips touched lightly, but they kissed deeply. Her eyes were closed as if giving him respite from their fatal influence on him. He knew he'd die one day; he knew it when she opened them again, because at that moment he discovered his vulnerability. "So much meaning in so little," he thought, while he grasped one of her despotic hands. His destiny fit in that fist; his whole life could be folded inside it. He cried as babies cry when they have nothing to do. He yielded to the feeling that he knew he couldn't control.

He belonged to her; he was the treasure her hands had been clasping for all these years.

"You don't need to listen to it all at once," she said in a half voice, and smiled at him.

*A cry is not suitable for prose, how to transmit the wetness of our emotions?*
*how to explain the language of our souls? A cry is not suitable for words.*
*Because when I wake up, thinking of you, weeping for you,*
*I don't want to go on writing pages, senselessly, in the book of my life,*
*I just want to cry and remember and hold that piece of happiness*
*that's fleeing away from me while I forget how to cry.*

## Chapter 49

Miguel had told his dream to Leo. It had been a long time since they last met; however, it didn't take them much time to update each other and to resume their relationship as if it had never been interrupted. The truth was that Luiza was going to marry Alonso in a month and their kid had already been born. She was a beautiful girl, very pink and delicate, and her blue eyes were as deep as her mother's. However, he'd messed it up a little when telling the whole story to Leo; he'd mixed reality with his thoughts and Leo had got it wrong. Miguel didn't blame his friend for thinking he was actually going to go back to Luiza and take care of her child; it actually struck him as a more coherent denouement for their story, were it not for the fact that she was still with Alonso.

"It's not your own blood," said Leo to Miguel. "Anyway, you've been lost lately; I wondered if Hellen was sucking the life out of you. I'm happy you're back to normal." That was the phrase Leo used to mean he'd missed a friend: "You've been lost." It wasn't as personal as saying "I've missed you," in the active form. The passive form of the phrase he used made it seem more impersonal, more manly than the more semantic phrase.

"What does it matter if the baby's not my own blood?" said Miguel, not wanting to make the effort to disabuse his friend of his mistake.

"I told you what I think; it's not your child; are you willing to defy nature's law by raising someone else's progeny?"

"But it's Luiza's child; it's part of her and I love her for that."

"You can love Luiza, but let the kid be taken care of by her father. You should rather think of your own wellbeing; think of having your own child. In the end, that's the aim of being in a couple."

"But if she has a child and I love her, then it's my child too."

"You're incorrigible; I gave you my opinion, take it or leave it. If you want to ensure that someone else's genes will prevail, then you can consider her your child. Anyway, I'm really happy to see you again."

"Thanks, me too," said Miguel, not really enthusiastically; he had deliberately avoided Leo for the last six months; although he kept in touch with him on Facebook. His desire to start breathing fresh air had unconsciously drawn him away from Leo, but now he was morally weakened by the circumstances and his dream. Maybe it meant that he still couldn't accept that she had a life without him and that she wasn't his anymore. But was he in love with the present Luiza or was he still harboring romantic feelings for the Luiza he'd abandoned years before? He was sure that the present Luiza stirred emotions in him, but what to make of these emotions? He only knew that a child suited Luiza and it had given a bloom to her face and a new vitality to her body. Now she looked as fertile and opulent as the earth. He felt there was no desire she could not absorb; all the desire of the world could be poured on her and she would absorb it and bear fruit.

But he still remembered how she had been years earlier. She'd been like a kid; she'd remember every single thing he said and remind him of it. How many things had he done halfheartedly in his life! And there she was, asking him only to fulfill his implicit promise to take her out to dance once a week, to always hug her and whisper nice words in her ear, to love her above everything else, to say she was the most beautiful woman he'd ever seen, to never leave her, to be there when she felt sad, to bring her flowers once in a while, to like everything she cooked, to cook for her whenever she visited him, to stay overnight whenever she felt lonely, to bring her coffee in bed, to make it strong enough so she'd wake up. That was all she'd asked from him, nothing more, but Miguel didn't understand the mechanism of happiness and he'd thought making her happy was too time-consuming. So he'd given her up.

Every day we play hide and seek, and we still haven't found ourselves,
we play at politics and economics, and at being masters of our lives, and
rules are necessary to keep the game going.
But today we play at writing our poems on a blank page,
as we played at making breakfast this same morning,
and we play at loving and hating, till our games become our profession,
and our poems are not a game anymore, and we love and hate in earnest.

Out of the same dust you were created
and in freedom you become one flesh
to be fruitful and multiply your love
born of steadfast justice and mercy.
And in a simple act, a "We accept" confirms
what was written in Heaven,
that a man shouldn't be alone,
that two souls pray better than one.
And so your heart may be aware
that you're content with Heaven's gift
you cry today "I take Thee,

bones of my bones, flesh of my flesh."

For from dust we came and to dust we'll return,

but while there's love, there's hope,

and while there's hope

there's life eternal.

## Chapter 50

Miguel was going to work by tram. It was early in the morning, when our
brains are still fresh and the dream world starts receding into reality. His
mind was free from worries other than how to endure eight hours of
confinement without breaking down. He was reading a book when he
suddenly heard a stentorian voice reciting some peace of literature. He
stopped reading and focused on the voice; it wasn't literature that he was
hearing but a description of an episode in a cartoon. The stentorian voice
came from a nine-year-old kid who, in order to make the story more
appealing to his classmates, was reciting it with all his might. The story
was about a ninja spider who fought against evil cockroaches who wanted
to take over the world with sly plans. The cockroaches had the advantage
that they could fly, but the spider could weave spider webs which allowed
it to fight the villains in the air. The spider, besides having mastered ninja
skills, was also versed in the Kung Fu arts, especially in the technique of
the drunk spider, which it had learned in a Shaolin temple. Some of the
kids thought that the ninja abilities were way superior to the Kung Fu
techniques the spider used to fight. They preferred it when the spider
disappeared in a cloud of smoke or threw ninja stars to when it started
contorting itself into weird Kung Fu positions. A strongly heated debate
ensued and opinions were divided. One of the kids asked Miguel, "What
do you think? Is ninja better than Kung Fu?"

Such a simple question couldn't be left unanswered and Miguel said:

"Ninja is the art of cunning, but Kung Fu is an inner force that can help you in any battle, physical or spiritual."

The debate seemed to have been concluded by this statement, but one of the kids argued back: "It's easy to talk about spiritual force when you're away from danger, but when you're in a real battle, and you fear your opponent has the upper hand, I'd like to see you resort to Kung Fu meditation to protect your mind while your ass is being kicked."

The advocates of ninja superiority roared in approval, while the Kung Fu supporters started to complain and counter attack erratically, some of them even giving up on the coherence of their logic by trying to undermine their opponents' stance with phrases such as: "Your mother prefers Kung Fu to ninja!" or "Why don't you ninjam a potato in your mouth and shut up!"

But Miguel wouldn't allow the discussion to descend into the type of argument people have over the sports pages, so he raised his voice to say: "I admit that the art of outsmarting a stronger opponent is very valuable, but most of the time our greatest opponent is ourselves."

Now everyone agreed that Miguel was right from an idealist point of view, but when a real situation of danger was considered, Miguel's theory was simple blabber. However, no one told this to Miguel and he felt as smart as ever.

"And who do you think is the second best fighter in the Ninja Spider?" asked one of the kids of Miguel.

"I've never watched that cartoon," said Miguel, and he might as well have said that he was a cosmonaut from Mars; it would've had the same effect on the kids. They stared at him in amazement for five seconds, the time they needed to reprocess the information they'd just received. At last one of them said: "You don't like the Ninja Spider?"

"I've never heard of it before," said Miguel, allowing himself to sink deeper into quicksand.

"What?! You must be joking!" was the only possible response the kid could think of without losing his mind.

By this point Miguel had realized the effect his words had on these kids, so he decided to deviate slightly from the truth, and he said: "Yes, the truth is my parents punished me for having bad grades by not allowing me to watch the Ninja Spider, so I couldn't watch a single episode."

The kids' faces went from bewilderment to plain indignation. They all related to Miguel and some of them started having psychosomatic reactions as soon as they heard him. One of the kids even cried a few tears.

"I hate your parents," one of the kids said. "If my parents did the same to me, I'd never speak to them again."

"Don't worry. I'll catch up later," said Miguel, trying to spare his parents the chagrin of being hated by this kid. "The punishment ends in one week."

"Ok, I'll tell you everything you've missed till now," said one of the kids magnanimously.

Miguel was on the point of answering when the teacher shouted: "Ok, we get off here."

Miguel returned his eyes to the book he was reading as soon as the kids started walking towards the tram door. However, twelve seconds after, he heard an anxious shout: "Miguel, what are you doing still on the tram? Get off right now!"

He looked around to see the kid who shared his name. It was astonishing for him to hear such a name in Poland, but "maybe it's some Spanish kid," he thought. However, he couldn't see any Spanish-looking kid around him. He at once spotted the shouting teacher and she was looking in his direction, so he turned around to see if for any reason there was a kid hiding behind him.

The teacher started coming towards him; she had to put her arm between the tram doors to stop them from closing. She got on and another teacher held the doors open for her so she'd have time to grab the kid and get off the tram. As she came towards him, Miguel had the strange sensation that she was becoming taller and taller. By the time she reached him, she was at least fifty centimeters taller than him. He was scared, but he got even more scared when she grabbed him by the wrist and, with an astonishing strength, led him off the tram.

Once they were on the sidewalk, she stared down at Miguel and told him: "What are you daydreaming about Miguel? We need to get to the zoo by eight o clock."

It was just after having seen all the animals in the zoo that Miguel woke up.

## Chapter 51: Death from love

When Miguel was a little kid, he used to spend his summers at his grandparents'. His grandfather was a congenial man and the atmosphere around him was always convivial. His grandfather had come from Paraguay and had experienced a lot of adventures. His life was furrowed by sorrows and joys. He'd shot a man back in Paraguay and he'd had romances all his way to Argentina. His grandpa had taught him to play chess. Miguel had played the first time with a classmate at primary school and she had won because, according to her rules, a pawn can't take the queen, so Miguel had to refrain from taking that valuable piece. When Miguel asked his grandpa to teach him how to play, he was astounded by the fact that a pawn can not only defeat a queen but also become one if he advances enough. It was a revolutionary idea, but unfortunately it came with the realization of the fact that he'd been outwitted by a girl.

Years later, when Miguel was past his teenage years and he was showing signs of manhood, he would go to visit his grandpa, who'd recently lost his wife, and listen to his stories.

"Yes my dear," said his grandfather looking straight at him with his dim gray eyes, "I was a success with girls." And at that moment Miguel realized how appealing those blue eyes must have been to girls and how difficult it must be for his grandfather to end his days alone.

"We used to go to dance and let me tell you something: the girl is always feeling the same as you do; the attraction is reciprocal." Miguel thought this aphorism must be true, coming from a man who had surely had his share of romantic experiences.

"We were dancing and we didn't wear briefs or boxers like nowadays; in those days we wore underpants. So, when in the middle of the dance you got a little excited, it was noticeable, you get it?" Miguel was just seeing an intimate confession coming and was trying by all means to dodge it. He tried to deviate from the train of thought with no success; he said, "And what did you use to dance?"

"All kinds of music", he said, settling Miguel's inquietude, "but always in couples. And the girl would seek to excite you, you know, and then she'd be your accomplice; she would slightly touch your leg with hers and then, as you couldn't go to sit in that state, she would shield you from everybody's sight thus preventing your embarrassment." Now Miguel started to see a point in all this; there was a little romance in his grandpa's stories after all; not everything concerned affairs with married women and girls he'd been with till he got them pregnant. He couldn't utter any comment anyway; he was just hoping this conversation would unexpectedly reach its end.

"Then you went to sit beside your girl and you proposed all kinds of things to her to see what she would accept, but sometimes she came with her mother and you just walked her back to her seat. Here's another thing

152

you must know: if you don't take your chance with a girl, she will talk bad about you and no other girl will want to be with you. But if you please that girl, you'll start building a good reputation among the other girls and then you will see them lining up to be with you." Miguel was definitely taking mental notes of everything by this time, though he was really wondering whether it was worthwhile trying to please every girl; he might as well try to speak every language on earth and achieve world peace in the meantime.

"Once a girl died of love for me, literally," his grandpa said and Miguel couldn't help smiling. He was pondering how distressing that dreadful gift of melting girls' hearts must be. "Really," the handsome old man said, at first smiling too but then trying to take a serious attitude towards the subject. His lips suddenly slackened and his eyes seemed to look with a solemn query at Miguel's. Miguel returned his grandpa's look as if assenting to the new tone the conversation had taken and tacitly allowed his grandpa to go on.

"I barely knew her, but I had invited her to a party and was going to fetch her home. We lived in the countryside and I went to her house on horseback. I came to the gate and had to open it and then close it without dismounting; it always took a certain time to perform this maneuver. At that moment, her mother must have seen me because I saw her coming out to meet me; she started calling out: Rose, Rose and she sent another daughter to go and tell her sister I was there. When I was drawing near the house I saw this girl was crying and telling something to her mother; I could also see the pale expression on her mother's face before she ran towards the house. I got off the horse and went to see what the matter was. The crying girl didn't know what had happened; she just told me gaspingly that her sister lay unconscious on the floor of her bedroom before resuming her crying. After a few eternal minutes, her mother came rushing out and told me: "Luis, Luis, my little darling, my Rose; she's suffered a heart attack; we've already called the doctor. I'm so sorry, but you should go home."

I went home with a burdened heart and a muddled mind. However, the day after the incident I learned exactly what had happened. Her mother came to see me; she needed to tell me something. The meeting didn't last longer than fifteen minutes, but the necessary words were uttered in less than a minute:

"My Rose was beautifully dressed up when you came; she'd done her hair and she was wearing makeup she'd borrowed from her older sister. We found her lying near the window. When I called out to her she must have looked through the window and she must have seen you. The doctor said she had a weak heart; we didn't know about it... Luis, her heart couldn't resist the emotion; she died instantly."

## Chapter 52

Miguel was dreaming again, and again it was so real. This time it was an aunt of his; he couldn't actually tell which one. It was an ideal aunt, a sexy blond blue-eyed one, or maybe green-eyed; he was colorblind in his dreams. She had a two-year-old child, who was playing on the carpet where Miguel was lying. Suddenly the aunt came to him and told him how happy she was to see him. He instinctively put his hands around her waist – the strange thing about dreams is that things generally evolve in the way we want them to – and she drew her body near to his and wrapped him in her arms. Her thighs were pressing against one of his legs and this gave him the cue to start kissing her. She kissed him back, leaning upon a table that happened to be around – every useful element happens to be around in dreams.

Miguel wasn't aware that he was creating his own porn scene in his head; for all he knew, he was actually living it. In this porn dream, the girl didn't get magically naked, as generally happens in some movies. There weren't close-ups of intimate parts either. The only close-up he felt necessary would be a shot of her thighs pressing against his legs, but it was a sensorial close-up rather than a visual one.

She told him they couldn't do it there because people might come in. Miguel suggested a bathroom, but she wasn't pleased with that idea. She left but came back almost instantly – in good dreams you don't need to be patient – and she told him she'd found a room they could use. The building looked like a school, full of rooms on both sides of a long hall. She entered one of the rooms and he followed her in; inside there was a plastic swimming pool where she was lying on a blanket. That room would probably serve as their love nest. When he was getting closer to her, a friend of hers entered and asked her what she was doing; it was evident he'd guessed what was happening so Miguel just took him by the arm and led him outside. However, the sneer on the friend's face predicted trouble. When Miguel and his aunt were again getting ready to submerge themselves in the empty swimming pool, a woman – maybe a teacher, if we continue with the school theme – knocked on the door. Miguel's aunt opened it and the woman asked her what kind of indecency she was perpetrating inside. When she threatened to come in, Miguel started to slither through a window that opened onto the hall. The window had a mosquito net which was torn at the bottom, where Miguel first wedged his head. Then he lay on the frame of the window, balancing on his stomach. In case the teacher went in, he'd have to raise his legs to slip forward and hopefully cushion the fall with his hands; otherwise, he'd just raise his head and fall back onto his feet. He was in this predicament when he woke up – fortunately, we can get into as much trouble as we want in a dream and solve it by simply switching it off. But what did this dream mean? He only knew it was a happy dream; there wasn't any trace on remorse in it. For a few seconds, the time it takes for reality to seep in, he regretted having woken up; he wanted to go back to that room. Finally, he resigned himself to his conscious life, but he was happy to feel that his libido had woken up again; he was again yearning for a woman, which meant that he might be at last ready to be in a relationship again.

That day Luiza's daughter, Mabel, was having her baptism and he was going to be the godfather. He wasn't a religious person, but he did like the idea of being in charge of her spiritual development; after all, that's the only kind of development that lasts us more than a lifetime. He was happy to meet Alonso at the church; he was grateful to that man for taking care of his dear Luiza. Because love is a tricky thing; it's not a feeling but an active state of the spirit. He felt that his soul had woken up and that his egotism was now muffled when he thought of Luiza. He didn't desire her physically; he just loved her and wished her well.

## Chapter 53

It was Leo's birthday and he couldn't find a better way to celebrate than smoking something in a public park. Miguel was reluctant to smoke during the day; he'd already yielded to Leo's invitation one afternoon when they went to buy ice-cream, but he couldn't keep himself from blinking frantically in front of the vendor; his eyes were too dry. But it was his birthday so Miguel accepted and took two drags. Then he declined to smoke further because he had something very important to do and he wanted to be sober. Half an hour before, when he'd gotten off the tram on his way to meet Leo, he'd needed some directions to know how to get to the park so he'd approached a pretty blonde who was selling seasonal fruit on a street stall. When he'd finished asking for directions, he just couldn't detach his eyes from her, the eyes he'd involuntarily opened wide as soon he'd seen her close up. Once in a decade, Miguel could say of a girl: "She's the most beautiful girl I've ever seen." and it wouldn't be a lie; this had been his once in a decade opportunity. But for him to be able to say it, he needed to establish at least an acquaintance with the girl;

otherwise, it would be too painful to admit he'd just fallen in love with a passerby. He had left the street stall because he wasn't the kind of person who acts spontaneously, but he'd rebuked himself for his lack of courage. However, he was never so hard on himself because he knew most of life's best gifts came gratuitously to him, so he'd decided to take it easy; he'd go and meet his friend and, if destiny wanted it, he'd find the girl at the same place when he came back.

Of course, after having two drags of Leo's smoke, Miguel proposed zealously to go back to that tram stop and then to go downtown or somewhere else. He also explained to Leo his reason for not smoking more: "I want my eyes to look as elegant as possible while I stake my heart on a girl's response. No one likes dying in rags." So Leo didn't insist any longer and he kindly agreed to go to the tram stop and then look for a place to eat.

When they got near the stall, Miguel asked Leo to wait somewhere else while he addressed his destiny. He approached the girl and was out of words, as he'd expected. He hadn't planned the conversation, but his objective was very simple: to ask for her Facebook. She was selling stuff, so the natural thing to do to gain time was to buy something, so he did, but to his surprise she was selling juicy and cheap tangerines, which he bought willingly. After she'd given him the bag and the business transaction was over, he cast the only anchor of his hopes: "Can I find you on Facebook?" he asked, and she nodded, a little abashed. So he went on: "So can you give it to me?" to which she responded this time with a yes and her full name. While he was writing it down on his phone and asking her to check the spelling, she asked him some questions and showed herself willing to strike up a conversation with him. This meant that by the time he'd finished writing her full name, he felt at ease with her, as if all of his doubts and pangs of anxiety had instantly vanished and now being friends with her was the most natural thing. She was friendly and as

157

pleasant as a girl can be which, combined with her beauty, put Miguel into a daydream he was afraid of waking up from.

No matter what, he was happy when he met Leo afterwards and when he went back home. Even if he didn't see her again, even if she had been nice to him just because it was in her nature, he was happy to have met her because he knew, once again, how it feels to be in love.

www.ingramcontent.com/pod-product-compliance
Lightning Source LLC
Chambersburg PA
CBHW071258130626
46556CB00003B/1371